Brian couldn
had the balls to challenge him. Between his friends and
family pussyfooting around him and the deference
which came with rank, it had to have been well before
the accident. He leaned forward, resting his palms on
the counter.

"What?"

Riley shrugged.

"Go ahead. Tell me what's on your mind.
Everyone else around here seems free to express their
opinion." He saw the baiting for what it was. Hell, he'd
practically begged for someone to snap back when he
growled instead of treating him like he was made of
spun glass.

She met his glare head on and held it, something
few people could do. "I was thinking you could benefit
from Asses Anonymous." She rounded off her verbal
jab by jutting out her chin.

"Really?" Despite the vow he'd made that morning
to steer clear of this intriguing woman, he obeyed the
call. Especially as she continued to challenge him.

"Sure, I mean a twelve-step program might take the
edge off all that sunshine and happiness you've been
sharing today."

Andrea,
Here's someting to
keep you busy this
summer. :-)

A Hero's Second Chance

by

Melissa Klein

Melissa Klein

A Hero's Second Chance

Cover Art by *Diana Carlile*

The Wild Rose Press, Inc.
PO Box 708
Adams Basin, NY 14410-0708
Visit us at www.thewildrosepress.com

Publishing History
First Edition, 2021
Trade Paperback ISBN 978-1-5092-3838-5
Digital ISBN 978-1-5092-3839-2

Previously Published: Her Hometown Hero 2014
Published in the United States of America

Dedication

This book is dedicated to my son, Daniel, my father, Jack, and other men and women in uniform. I'm humbled by your sacrifice, awed by your bravery, and proud to be among those who with open arms welcome you home.

Chapter One

Riley Logan pulled into the mall parking lot and killed the engine of her 60's muscle car. Seeing only a few other vehicles, she fished her phone out of her purse to check the time.

Too early to get going and too late to back out.

Having already dropped Gloria's rag top, she lifted her face and soaked in the sun's warmth.

What would Jake think about me using his car in the parade.

Riley shook her head to stop the downward spiral of remembering and longing.

It's time to get on with my life.

Some days were easier than others. After a moment she flipped the latch on the glove box and pulled out a dog-eared paperback she'd bought at a second-hand bookstore, and in seconds she was lost in the southern gothic novel.

"That is some kinda sweet ride."

The southern drawl jolted Riley out of the fictional world. She bit back a yelp, angry at herself for letting someone get close without her noticing. Even if she was in the relative safety of a suburban Atlanta mall, it was never a good idea for a woman to let down her defenses. Jake, who'd seen more than his fair share of violence as a cop, had drilled that into her.

Riley craned her neck towards the voice. Grant

Davis, the owner of Davis Air Transport where she worked, planted his hands on the top of the door. Something short of lust sparkled in the man's blue eyes, but the look wasn't for her. Gloria had that effect on men.

She stroked the car's steering wheel. "68 was a great year."

"Classic." Grant popped the door handle with a mile-wide grin on his face. "I can't believe you actually agreed to let me borrow her for the parade."

Back in Ohio, she'd barely known her co-workers' names, but here Riley enjoyed the good-natured teasing at Davis Air Transport. "Nice try, Boss." She shot him a look: half smile, half I'm-totally-serious-about this. "That was never the plan. I'll see to it your hero makes it down the parade route in one piece."

She'd driven Jake's cherry-red convertible to work one day when her compact wouldn't start. After that Grant hounded her until she agreed to let the town council use Gloria for Magnolia Springs's Memorial Day parade. Riley was ferrying their hometown hero the mile-long stretch of Piedmont Street.

Grant opened his mouth at her rebuff as if to argue with her. Until pretty, blond Abby Davis slipped up behind him. Dressed in white shorts and a cute patriotic top, Abby smiled at her husband. Then she hip-checked him out of the way and leaned over to wrap her arms around Riley's shoulders. "Is he giving you a hard time?"

She tensed for a moment before relaxing into the inevitable hug. "No more than usual."

The boss's wife released her from the embrace with a squeeze to her shoulders. Abby had shown up at

Riley's tiny house with a welcome basket on her arm and an invitation to dinner on her lips. She hadn't taken the woman up on her offer. After years of being on her own, she found it difficult to open to people. That didn't mean she didn't appreciate the effort. That was why she volunteered to put Gloria and herself on display. This couple and a few others welcomed her, so she owed them.

Grant patted her hand, drawing her to the here and now. "You win this time, but don't think I've given up." He wrapped an arm around Abby and planted a kiss on her cheek. With a smirk for Riley, he wandered over to a group of men admiring a powder blue Mustang that had pulled into the parking lot.

"Boys and their toys. If it goes fast, he drives, rides, or flies it." Abby shook her head. "Do you want to know why Grant has a thing for your car?"

Abby's smile piqued her curiosity. "You have the key to understanding the male fascination with muscle cars?"

Abby stroked the white leather. "He told me something pretty special happened for the first time in the backseat of a car like this one."

Riley screwed up her face. *Jeez!* That was way more information than she ever needed to know about her boss. Mercifully, Abby moved on to safer topics of conversation.

"You are coming to the company picnic."

Davis Air Transport employed about twenty pilots, mechanics, and office workers. Grant treated his people more like family than employees. The Memorial Day picnic was the second company gathering in the three months she'd been working there. Riley loved her job and the people she worked with, but as much as she wanted to put down roots here, her people skills ran closer to hermit than social butterfly. Riding in a parade and having several hundred people staring at her was as much socializing as she could handle in one day.

Feigning nonchalance instead of the awkwardness she really felt, she shrugged. "I hadn't planned on it. I thought I might head over to the hangar and get caught up on some work."

Abby pursed her lips. "It's a holiday. You should be out having some fun, not toiling away for that slave-driver you work for." With a grin, she fisted her hands against her hips. "I won't take no for an answer."

More of Jake's wisdom echoed in her ears. "How are you ever going to meet people if you shut yourself up in your house all the time?" He'd often asked the question when she balked at doing things with his police buddies. He was right. It was time she started putting herself out there. "Okay, I'll come."

Riley took a mental inventory of her cupboards for something she could contribute to the picnic and came up empty. The power bars and Lean Cuisines she lived on weren't going to cut it. There was one thing she had and it would be more appreciated by the boss than her attempting potato salad. Touching Abby on the arm, she shot the lady a grin. "What do you say after the parade you and Grant take Gloria for a spin?"

****

"You know, I'd rather be water boarded than do this." Brian Stone raked his fingers over his cropped hair.

How have I let myself get roped into this?

His words bounced off Grant, who'd crossed the

mall parking lot where he'd been admiring a line of classic cars. Grant arched an eyebrow and grinned. "Well, it's your own damned fault. Quit earning Purple Hearts and the town council won't make you do this anymore."

Brian shot the guy an eat-shit glare as Grant worked the buttons on his jacket. It wasn't that he didn't appreciate what the town was doing. He didn't see himself as a hero. The medic who'd kept him from bleeding out … now that guy was a hero. And the physical therapist who'd put up with his attitude, she was a hero. All he had managed to do was—survive. Pure stubbornness and tenacity didn't make a man a hero.

Grant knocked Brian's hands out of the way and took over the job of getting him trussed up in his dress blues. Since the IED had exploded under his Humvee, his grasp wasn't as strong as it used to be.

With the job done, Grant stepped back and gave him the tip-to-tails onceover. "You look pretty good."

Considering was implied. He was half the man he'd been a year ago. Not only in muscle mass and weight but between the ears as well. Other than taking up space at his sister's house and playing video games with his niece and nephew, he hadn't done jack since he'd returned to Magnolia Springs.

With his uniform squared away, they headed to the parade starting point. Grant shot him one of his smart-ass grins. For the past thirty years the two of them had gotten themselves into more situations than he cared to remember, so he knew that look.

Grant shoved his hands in his pockets as his grin widened. "You're about to be very glad you said yes to being the grand marshal."

The guys stopped by the sweetest ride Brian had seen in a long time. A cherry-red convertible gleamed and propped against the front quarter panel rested a fine specimen of the female persuasion. Her long, nearly black hair fell in a straight shot to the middle of her back and if that wasn't enough to get his attention … long, sun-kissed legs jutted out of a pair of denim shorts. Back in the day, he would have been jonesing to catch a ride with this knockout.

Grant made the introductions. "I'd like you to meet my wingman, Lieutenant Colonel Brian Stone." Grant thumbed in his direction. "Brainstorm is the only man on planet Earth more likely to take a dare than me."

He kept the cringe to himself.

Not anymore.

His days of skydiving and motorcycle racing were over. Along with his military career.

Grant clapped him on the shoulder, drawing him closer to the woman. "B.S., I'd like you to meet Riley Logan. She's come on board to help Maggie out with some of the bookkeeping."

Brian scrubbed his palm against his pants leg before clasping the hand she offered. "Nice to meet you."

Her small smile made him want to say something clever to see if he could coax out a bigger one. "Watch out for my little sister. She'll work you to death if you let her. I should know. She's been bossing me around since she was old enough to talk."

A lovely blush bloomed on her prominent cheeks, turning her honey-colored skin a warm shade of pink. "I'll keep that in mind." Her gaze met his for the briefest second before she ducked her head.

That split second was all the time he needed to register the violet color of her eyes, piercing, like Elizabeth Taylor's. With such a lyrical voice and arresting eyes, she could have easily been one of the Sirens. Then she kicked off the car's quarter panel where she'd been leaning and moved around the front of the car. Quick and sleek, she moved like an athlete.

"We're about ready to get started Colonel Stone if you'll take your seat." Riley gestured towards the folded-up ragtop where someone had draped a red and blue quilt.

Like a smack upside the head, Brian's attention snapped back to the job ahead. His stomach twisted thinking about having to perch on the back of that car so the townspeople could wave and cheer.

And heap praises on him he didn't deserve.

With her passenger settled in, she headed towards their spot in the parade. One of the mechanics from work motioned her behind the color guard using hand signals as if she were bringing a jet in for a landing. When he crossed his arms, Riley put the car in park.

With a broad smile, the middle-aged man approached the rear of the car, clasping Colonel Stone on the shoulder as he took his hand. "Welcome home, Brian. Our town is mighty proud of you."

In stark contrast to the man's enthusiasm, the colonel's expression remained impassive. Several seconds of silence past. "Thanks, Truck."

Caught off guard by the colonel's cool response, she twisted in her seat and stared. Having a sense of belonging, to even one person, was what Riley longed for. Here he was stiff and unfeeling as if the town's collective embrace had little meaning.

After patting Colonel Stone on the shoulder again, Truck took a step away from the car. "Well, if you or Maggie need anything, just let us know." Emotion colored his voice.

Then he leaned across the passenger side door. "I'm going to check on the rest of the parade. It looks like we'll be ready to start as soon as the Shriners and the fire department get settled in."

Then she was alone with her sullen parade marshal. Anxious to get things moving as quickly as possible, she gripped the steering wheel with both hands. Several minutes passed where only the sound of a marching band tuning up filled the awkwardness between them. Riley tried to think of something to say that wasn't along the lines of, "What's wrong with you?" When she came up empty handed, she tilted the rearview mirror so she could get another look at Mr. Big Shot. He had a commanding air that drew her attention and held it. He wasn't Hollywood handsome. His features were too angular with a strong brow, square jaw, and deep-set eyes. And that scowl. *Damn.* She wanted to ask what prompted him to participate in the parade when he clearly didn't want to.

Before Riley could voice her question, Truck gave them the go-ahead sign. She started the car and eased forward as the parade began. She and her passenger were the third in line, behind a banner held by two high stepping majorettes and the Boy Scout color guard. She chuckled to herself as the two young boys worked to hold up flags nearly twice their size.

As they moved down Piedmont Street, Riley observed the crowds lining either side. An unbroken line of people clad almost exclusively in red, white, and blue waved and called out to her passenger. The only thing missing from this scene was for the crowd to toss laurel wreaths.

She shot a quick glance backwards. Colonel Stone sat ramrod straight, jaw clenched, hands fisting the quilt.

Jeez, did nothing affect this man?

Finally, Riley's mouth got the better of her. "I think you're supposed to wave."

He responded with a robotic wave that only made him seem more the conquering hero.

Riley wished her arms were long enough so she could cuff the back of this guy's head for his less than gracious attitude. "Would it kill you to smile?"

He shifted stiffly in his seat. "Either that or the heat will. It's hotter than five yards of Afghan sand propped up on this car."

Okay, so maybe she should cut him some slack. She leaned down and flipped open a cooler. "Sorry. Have some bottled water."

Keeping one eye on the Boy Scouts in front of her, she reached backward. Their fingers met, sending her pulse into overdrive at the contact. His hands were surprisingly gentle as he eased the bottle from her grasp.

He cracked the lid and drank heavily. "Thanks…That hit the spot."

Riley focused on the road ahead, determined to ignore the surge of excitement coursing through her. Sure, it had been three years since she'd felt the touch of a man's hands, but that didn't mean she could go all gaga over a minor, inconsequential touch.

Then an elderly man in his dress uniform worked his way out of a folding chair, capturing her full attention. Riley gripped the steering wheel as the man offered Colonel Stone a smart salute. Her throat tightened with emotion. Cutting her eyes to the rearview mirror, she checked the colonel's reaction. Surely, if his jaw had been any tighter, his teeth would have cracked. She held her breath.

"Stop."

She did, her pulse thrumming in her veins.

He eased to his feet nearly as stiffly as the elderly man. The crowd on both sides of the street grew quiet as the colonel drew to attention and snapped a returning salute.

For several heartbeats everyone seemed frozen in a Norman Rockwell painting. Then as quickly as the touching scene began, it ended. The colonel returned to his perch, the crowd resumed cheering, and the parade went on.

"So, you're new in town."

Her gaze shot to the rearview mirror again, seeing him wave with a little more energy. "I've been here about three months. How'd you know?"

"Around here everybody's either related to or goes to church with everybody else, so new people tend to stick out."

Riley nodded. She'd trod the path of the outsider many times. Hopefully, friendships would come and if they didn't, she was comfortable with her own company. The parade crawled forward another few feet, him waving and her watching the road ahead.

"Hey, keep talking to me." The colonel leaned across the back seat to clasp her on the shoulder, sending sparks through her body. "It keeps my mind off me sitting up here like a homecoming queen." As he shifted around on his seat, the creases at the corners of his eyes deepened.

Riley racked her brain for something to say. "I'm not much of a talker." A childhood spent keeping secrets and long stretches of adulthood spent alone hadn't done much to alter her natural shyness.

"I can see that. Tell me about yourself. How'd you end up working for Grant?"

She'd accepted the bookkeeping job, hoping for a fresh start in a place free of painful memories. A new career, a new town, and hopefully a new life. Way too much information. "He hired me." Would that stop the twenty questions?

Brian snorted a laugh. "Boy, you are a woman of few words. How do you get along with my sister? Maggie talks a thousand words a minute."

Riley hid a smile. At first she'd been intimidated by Maggie's dynamic personality, but after a few weeks she'd come to like the woman, even if she still made Riley's head spin sometimes. "We get along just fine, thank you."

"Tell me about your car. You clearly weren't old enough to drive during the 60s, so how'd you end up with a muscle car?"

When she packed up and headed south, memories and that car had been the only thing of Jake's she'd kept. Riley worked to keep her voice even. "She was my husband's. He bought her when he became a detective on the Cincinnati police force."

Brian's gaze moved over Gloria as his hand caressed her leather seat. "She's a real beauty."

"Thanks." She answered on her late husband's behalf.

They lapsed into a silence that wasn't nearly as thick with tension as it had been at the beginning of the parade. Every minute or so, she glanced back at the soldier. After the way he reacted to the veteran's salute, she reevaluated her opinion of him. Even if his heart wasn't made of stone, he still wasn't the kind of guy she'd want to spend tons of time with. The darkness that oozed from him came too close to her own to make her comfortable around him.

Finally, they reached the end of the parade route, and she pulled into the supermarket parking lot. Before Riley could park, Brian flipped up the passenger seat and was easing out of the car. As he worked his way past the seat, he came close enough she felt heat radiating off his body. He smelled of spicy aftershave and good clean man sweat, a combination that brought back pleasant memories.

She held her breath, hoping to cut off the colonel's masculine scent as well as the memories they induced. He cleared the car. "If you'll wait, Truck will be along in a second to take you back to the mall."

He turned but didn't respond to her statement. Instead, his gaze worked its way over her, sending a shot of electricity up her spine.

Riley ducked her chin. Before she'd begun studiously examining her fingernails, she'd gotten a good second look at him. His eyes were hazel rather than brown as she'd originally thought and his lips were full and curled into a pleasant smile that softened the harshness of his face.

As quickly as his smile formed, it disappeared

behind a scowl. "Thanks for the ride."

"Aren't you going to wait for Truck?"

Chapter Two

Brian shoved away from the car and the beautiful woman behind the wheel. "That's okay. I could use the walk." He turned, heading who-the-fuck-knew-where. Staring into her violet eyes, he'd almost forgotten the past twelve months. Instead, he imagined himself sitting next to her as they flew down the road, her dark hair blowing in the breeze. But forgetting wasn't an option.

He moved as quickly as his busted-up body would let him. Then at the edge of the parking lot, he stopped. The urge to look over his shoulder clawed at him. That was an impulse he didn't need to obey. Not only was it a bad idea for him to want something he shouldn't have, but he also didn't need another look to have her indelibly imprinted on his brain.

Minutes later his wandering took him to his old high school. He stopped at the edge of the long expanse of turf, the backdrop of his youth. It seemed at least a hundred years ago that he'd been BMOC. Football, baseball, track, he'd done it all. And it had come so goddamned easy. Back then his body did what he told it to. His physical prowess hadn't ended there. All those years in the army, he found he could hump a heavier pack or pound the ground for more miles than men twenty years younger.

"Jesus H. Christ. I thought I was going to have to

call out the National Guard to find your ass. What are you doing here?"

He shrugged. "Beats the hell out of me."

Grant thumbed over his shoulder to his truck. "Well, come on. Your sister is going to hand me my head if I don't get you over to the park. She said something about you helping out at the fund raiser."

Brian hauled himself into the truck, grunts of exertion and creaking bones making it an inelegant, noisy process.

"Damn… You move like an old man."

He snorted a laugh as he adjusted himself in the seat. "That's good, 'cause most of the time I feel like one."

Grant paused with his hand on the gearshift. "You taking something for the pain?"

Brian waved him off. He'd stopped the pain meds while still in the hospital back in Germany. Not so much because he'd been concerned about getting addicted. He wanted the pain as a reminder. "Nah, I can handle it."

"Suit yourself." Grant shrugged and put the truck in gear.

"I usually do." He'd been a self-centered bastard for the past year.

That was until Riley had gotten his attention. Her verbal kick in the pants made him see the overwhelming but heartfelt display of patriotism had little to do with how the town perceived him. Or even how he saw himself. The ride was about the soldiers who weren't there to receive their due. The reality check hadn't made the parade any easier, but then again he wasn't looking for easy.

After a couple blocks Grant asked, "What ya say we head to Cowboy's tonight after the fireworks? We could shoot some pool, drink a few beers. You know like in the old days. It's been a long time since I saw Brainstorm in action."

Man, they'd chased some tail back in the day, but now he could file that under not going to happen anymore. He doubted any sane woman would spend more than five minutes with a fucked-up mess like him and that was before they found out what the IED had done to his body. "Thanks, but I'll take a pass."

"It's all good." Grant shrugged. "What did you think of Riley? Pretty isn't she and that car of hers, *damn.*"

When Brian cocked an eyebrow at his buddy, Grant raised his hands in surrender. "Abby was the one who mentioned the two of you should meet. She thought since Riley's such a sweet, easy-going lady, you guys would have fun hanging out."

Sweet and easy-going were not the words that popped into his mind when he thought of Riley. Sharp wit and tight body fit the woman he'd run up against. Watching her slide behind the wheel of her car, all long tanned legs and sculpted arms, had been an exercise in self-control. Then halfway down the parade route, she'd pulled her long, nearly black hair into a ponytail. He'd been attempting to keep his gaze ahead until out of the corner of his eye, he caught a bead of sweat work its way down her neck. He'd had to grip the back of the seat to keep from leaning over to capture that droplet with his tongue.

Grant prodded his arm. "Hey man… you in there?"

"What?"

"God, I'd give a million bucks to know where your mind was just now." Grant laughed. "I asked if you wanted me to drop you back at your place. I'm kinda thinking that might be a good idea since you don't look right."

He shot a grin at his buddy. "Nah, I'm good. Maggie will chop me off at the knees if I don't show up to help her out."

Grant's expression darkened. Then he turned onto the road leading to the park without commenting on Brian's attempt at humor.

****

Hours after the parade, Riley found herself under an oak tree in Greenfield Park. Grant and Abby had taken her up on the offer to take Gloria for a spin. After dropping her off at her home, they'd driven around town for an hour or so then come back to pick her up. She'd tried once again to refuse the invitation to join them for the picnic. Her excuses had been ignored.

"If I eat another bite, I'll explode." Grant collapsed on the quilt Abby had spread out for their picnic.

She tugged the fried chicken leg out of Grant's hand. "Well, we can't have you exploding, can we?" She gave him a playful peck on the lips.

So, here she was. Not quite a third wheel since Abby's tale of running a 10k called The Magnolia Miles that morning and Grant's account of his pleasure cruise behind Gloria's wheel made her feel included as well as entertained. But it was time to leave.

She began collecting the paper plates, napkins, and cans of soft drink from the picnic. "Abby, everything was wonderful." Riley stopped mid-tidy when Grant leapt to his feet. A statuesque blond and a little girl approached their picnic spot.

Grant, who she'd seen ream out a pilot for failing to follow company protocol, bent on one knee and combed his fingers through the girl's golden curls. "Hi, precious. How's Daddy's girl?" He turned to her, a mile-wide grin on his face. "This is my daughter, Grace." The way he spoke her name sounded like a prayer.

"Hi, Grace." The wave the little girl offered had her heart thudding in her chest. Dressed in a red star-spangled sundress, white sandals, and blue bows, Grace looked like a patriotic angel.

"Heather, I'd like you to meet Riley Logan."

At the sound of her name, she tore her eyes from Grace.

Grant grinned as he continued with the introductions. "Not only is Riley a fabulous bookkeeper, but she's also generous with her automobiles."

Heather extended a slim, manicured hand. "Nice to meet you. I'm Grace's mom."

She glanced at the girl who'd skipped over to stand next to Abby. "She's beautiful."

"Thanks." Heather turned to Grant. "I'll pick her up in the morning."

Grant took Grace's hand. "Come on, Goldilocks. Let's go play a game."

Riley loved kids, especially the little ones. At Bethany Children's Home, where she'd lived from age ten, she'd always volunteered to watch the younger ones. Being childless hadn't been her idea or Jake's. Her heart ached as she said her goodbyes. "Thanks for including me in your picnic."

"Any time." Abby drew her in for another hug.

Riley picked her way through the patchwork of picnickers. On the far side of the creek which meandered through the park, lay the white, open-sided tent. She took the foot bridge which connected the two halves of the park, her shoes making rhythmic thuds as she stepped over the wooden planks.

Midway across the ten-foot span, she spotted the man who'd harried her thoughts all day. He'd changed from his uniform into a T-shirt and jeans and sat in one of the folding chairs clustered in the tent's shade. A ball cap kept her guessing at the color of his closely cropped hair but let her fully see the piercing stare as he tracked her movements.

Like a rabbit caught outside its hutch, Riley felt the urge to scamper into the safety of the tent. Which was ridiculous. He was simply a man, not a wolf in casual wear. He was nothing to her. She forced her stride to a slower pace and returned his gaze.

He stood as she reached the back of the tent. The lack of uniform did nothing to lessen his commanding presence. Everything, from the way his T-shirt stretched across his broad shoulders to the intensity of his stare, screamed power.

She paused. As he had earlier when he'd stood with his hands resting on Gloria's door, he seemed on the verge of saying something. Her breath quickened.

"Riley." Her name was squealed and in a pair of seconds a small body ran head long into hers.

"Hi, Lexi." Sticky hands snaked around her waist. "How much cotton candy have you had today?" The intense moment between Brian and her past. She looked down at Maggie Daniels's daughter.

"Only one bag." The seven-year-old grinned, her face tinged a bright pink. "Uncle Brian bought it for me."

An indulgent smile replaced the glare he'd given her.

Before she could spend too much time considering their mercurial uncle, she bumped knuckles with twelve-year-old, Matt. "Are you helping your mom?"

Lexi tugged at Riley's shirt, her expression as stern as any CEO's. "We were, but Mom said Matt was drinking up all the profits."

One look at Matt's expression and she bit back her laugh.

"I was not." He shoved his fists in the pockets of his shorts and kicked the ground.

Hearing the disagreement, Brian joined them. His gaze shot to Riley for an instant before he scrubbed his hand over his nephew's head. "We can't have that wild man. I guess you'll have to hang back here with me."

She learned from Maggie, Colonel Stone had been living with her and the kids since he retired from the army. It looked as if he was also acting as surrogate for the kids' absentee father.

Matt followed his uncle for a couple strides before turning back. "I almost forgot. Mom asked me to give you this." He handed her the bronze medal she'd won running the 10K.

Riley used that morning's race as practice for the one she'd run in Atlanta on the 4th of July. All through her twenties and thirties, she'd run long distance races. She'd even finished a couple marathons and a triathlon. Now, 10k was plenty long enough.

Matt turned to his uncle who was once again

studying Riley from sunglasses to sandals. "She's fast. Only two other people beat her and one of those was a super-fast girl from Kenya."

Brian raised an eyebrow. "Really?"

Her cheeks burned as she shoved it in her pocket. A third-place prize hardly compared to the chest full of medals he'd worn on his uniform. "It's no big deal." She gave Matt a pat on the shoulder. "I better go see what I can do to help your mom."

She edged her way past crates of lemons, heading for the woman she was beginning to think of as a friend, a first in longer than she cared to think about. "I came early thinking you might need the help."

Maggie turned from the industrial-size juicer she was operating. "Thank God. I'm up to my eyeballs in lemons."

"Where do you want me? I can take orders or keep the supply lines going."

Folding tables fenced three sides of the tent, giving the volunteers inside a narrow but shaded place to work. Directly ahead, a pair of women were busy taking orders, collecting money, and handing out cups of icy lemonade. It looked as if Victory for Veterans was doing a brisk business. That wasn't a big surprise given the day's temperature and the number of people gathered in the park.

Maggie didn't answer right away. Instead, something outside the tent captured her attention. The rising sounds of kids playing drew her attention as well. The colonel and Maggie's kids were tossing a ball around. Lexi bounced on spring loaded legs as Matt wound up an exaggerated pitch.

Many of Riley's childhood fantasies revolved

around something close to this scene, an adult who cared and a sibling to play with. But furrows line Maggie's brow. While she debated on whether to ask what had her friend worried, a shout for more lemonade came from the front of the concession stand.

Maggie jolted then called over her shoulder. "I'm on it."

"Why don't you take a break? I got this."

Maggie shot another glance towards the trio playing outside then shook her head. "I'm good. Why don't you help out up front?" She raised wet hands that were red from the acidic lemon juice. "No sense in both of us ending up a mess."

In seconds, the frenzy of taking orders and handling customers absorbed her attention. Eventually the line in front of the tent dwindled and Riley let the two other women leave to join their families. She spent the lull wiping down the makeshift counter and counting the till. They'd surpassed their goal by a couple hundred dollars, so she stepped to the back of the tent meaning to have a quick chat about expanding their charitable plans.

Maggie studied Brian and her kids. The three, now armed with gloves, had fanned out and were tossing the baseball between them. Matt's stance was wide and the boy was obviously taking the game seriously as he threw the ball to his uncle.

"Hold your glove up a little more."

"Got it," Matt corrected his stance.

Brian sent in a hard pitch which Matt caught. "That's it. Look out Tom Glavin, here comes Mighty Matt." His joke and the smile that accompanied it had them all beaming, Riley included. "Now send one over to your sister." When Matt reared back, Brian cautioned, "Not too hard."

She checked over her shoulder to see there were no customers then stepped over to where Maggie was propped against one of the folding tables. "You've got great kids."

Maggie offered Riley a warm smile. "Thanks, they sure love their uncle."

They both turned their attention to the game. "It looks like the feeling's mutual."

"He's good for them. They don't see their father much, so Brian's kinda filling in the holes."

The joy emanating from the kids engulfed her, drawing her into the interplay. She called to Lexi. "Give it all you've got."

The girl threw the ball wildly and the colonel extended his body to make the catch. He'd have easily caught the ball, except instead of stepping with his left leg to counterbalance his reach, his feet stayed anchored.

Three gasps went out as Brian hit the ground, followed by Maggie vaulting over the side of the concession stand. After sending at glare in his sister's direction, Matt threw down his glove and scrambled to his uncle's side.

Brushing aside Matt and Maggie's help, Brian struggled to his feet. His expression darkened, like a barely banked thunderstorm. She braced herself, expecting him to lash out at his family. Her heart clenched especially for Lexi who was sobbing.

After taking a couple awkward strides to his niece, Brian cupped the little girl's chin, thumbing away her tears. Lexi nodded to whatever Brian murmured to her then let Matt take her in the direction of a nearby playground.

Riley retreated further into the tent, partly to let Brian regroup without another person hovering but also wanting to cover the shame at causing the incident. Having earlier seen the Purple Heart pinned to his chest, she knew he'd been injured. She'd had no inkling his injuries were extensive enough to warrant that level of reaction from his family. Why then was he playing with his niece and nephew?

Prompted by raised voices, she shot a quick glance in Maggie and Brian's direction. His deep scowl caused a wave of sympathy for her friend. She doubted the confrontation would turn violent, but that didn't mean the words he used on Maggie wouldn't hurt. As she debated what to do, a family appeared at the front of the concession stand. With another glance behind her, Riley moved to the front of the tent to wait on them. Her hands might have been busy, but it wasn't enough distraction to prevent her from hearing the growled words coming from the back of the tent.

"You all right?"

Brian took a second to brush a bit of grass that still clung to his jeans. "Of course. I fell on grass for Christsake."

Ignoring his assurance, she clasped his elbow and tugged him towards the chairs. He shrugged her off, turning his back to her. "I'm fine." His temper ratcheted up a notch.

"I know. It's just…" She touched his arm again to get his attention.

He held out, not wanting to see that familiar look. When she didn't take her hand away, he finally caved and met her gaze. Yep, there it was—pity.

"Why didn't you want to go out with Grant? I think it would do you good."

Leaving one well-trod topic for another. Brian snatched the ball cap off his head and raked his fingers through his hair. Revisiting old haunts wasn't going to make him into the man he'd once been. And God knew he didn't need a reminder of how he once could snap his fingers and have a woman on each arm. That was so not a conversation he wanted to have with his sister. "Because I don't want to."

"I'm trying to help." Her voice broke with emotion.

God knew she was. She'd done everything but cut his meat for him. It was time to put an end to this for both their sakes. Otherwise, she'd grow to hate him. "I don't want your help. Stop hovering like a mother hen. I'm not one of your kids."

He turned on his heels, not wanting to see the hurt his angry words had caused. He took off towards the parking lot, running away for the second time today. As he crossed in front of the concession stand, he felt rather than saw Riley's gaze boring into him. He cut his eyes at her as he strode past, and the look on her face put the brakes on his retreat. Since he'd often seen the same harsh expression staring back at him in the mirror, he recognized the loathing that turned her lovely features to stone. Clearly, she'd witnessed the whole humpty-fucking-dumpty scene, including his follow-up imitation of a jackass. As much as he wanted to blow past her and escape to curse his temper and stupidity, his feet had other ideas.

She crossed her arms as he approached.

He couldn't remember the last time someone had the balls to challenge him. Between his friends and family pussyfooting around him and the deference which came with rank, it had to have been well before the accident. He leaned forward, resting his palms on the counter.

What?"

She shrugged.

"Go ahead. Tell me what's on your mind. Everyone else around here seems free to express their opinion." He saw the baiting for what it was. Hell, he'd practically begged for someone to snap back when he growled instead of treating him like he was made of spun glass.

She met his glare head on and held it, something few people could do. "I was thinking you could benefit from Asses Anonymous." She rounded off her verbal jab by jutting out her chin.

"Really." Despite the vow he'd made that morning to steer clear of this intriguing woman, he obeyed the call. Especially as she continued to challenge him.

"Sure, I mean a twelve-step program might take the edge off all that sunshine and happiness you've been sharing today."

Chapter Three

Riley could pick out the flecks of gold in Colonel Stone's hazel eyes as he closed the little distance between them. How had she gone from *thinking* he could use a personality transplant to voicing her opinion? At least she could have been a little more tactful. Between his aggressive stance and heated stare, he was fully capable of verbally eviscerating her. She braced for the blowback.

Instead, a deep rumbling laugh erupted from his lips. "You may be a woman of few words, but damn, the ones you do use are a kick in the pants." His humor exploded into a full-scale belly laugh.

Riley pulled away from his overwhelming presence as relief turned into embarrassment. "I'm not usually this blunt. My mouth got the better of me." She rubbed the back of her neck as if she was getting whiplash from trying to keep up with the guy's moods.

Brian's eyes softened. "Not a problem. You obviously care about my family and that makes you all right by me." Once again he invaded her personal space, sending her pulse into overdrive. "The first step to recovery is admitting you have a problem." His lips spread into a wicked grin. "I am an ass."

He shot a glance to the back of the tent. "Give me a second, and I'll come back to give you a hand." With a quick grip on her shoulder, he did an about-face and stalked off, all evidence of the fall gone.

After that mind-bending encounter Riley's mind swam in a pool of confusion, emotion, and hormones. She took several deep breaths then glanced around the concession stand for something to keep from spending too much time wondering what another round with Brian Stone would be like. It wouldn't be boring, that was certain.

She'd finished rearranging a stack of plastic cups when he approached from behind. His well-muscled arm brushed against hers as he eased to her side at the narrow serving area. Heat radiated from the contact point as if she'd been standing in the Georgia sun all day. She took a sip from her water bottle to quench the sensation now coursing through her veins. Never had a man's physical presence affected her like this.

"I may have gotten the steps out of order, but I'm pretty sure one of them is making amends." The teasing lilt of his voice did nothing to settle her nerves.

Riley followed his line of sight to Maggie, who was closing the production end of the concession stand. She looked at her brother, shooting him a smile. Brian nodded then turned to Riley. "Are we square now?"

Why did her opinion matter to him? It wasn't as if they were friends. She nodded anyway. "We're good."

A surge of late afternoon customers made any further conversation impossible until the sun set. Which was just as well since she seemed to be intent on demonstrating her lack of people skills every time she opened her mouth. Thank heaven, working near this man was a one-time only deal. Besides worrying about having another attack of open-mouth-insert-foot, the attraction for the colonel made her head swim.

After the rush of customers, Riley was forced to face the man who dominated their small space. She found him arms crossed, head cocked, and studying her. "What?" She ran her hand across her cheek. "Do I have something on my face?"

"You're perfect." He smiled. "I was wondering, other than the fact few can resist my sister's force of will, what made you get involved with Victory for Veterans. Is anyone in your family in the military?"

Jeez, in addition to nervous awareness, she also had to make small talk. The only thing worse than talking to a near stranger was talking about herself to a man who made her mouth dry and her pulse race as if she'd been running a marathon. Riley shrugged. "I wanted to help. It's a good cause." She kept back her initial motivation had been to ease some of her loneliness. The belief in the cause came as she saw how much the charity helped.

Brian nodded. "That it is."

A lone Roman candle exploding in the darkening sky signaled she could close for the night. The townspeople would be more interested in watching the fireworks display than buying drinks. Riley let out a relieved breath. Not only was she going to escape this man's probing questions, but she could also shoo him off without seeming rude. "Catch up with Maggie and the kids. I can finish up here."

His brow furrowed. "Don't you have some friends or family you could be hanging out with?"

Riley folded her arms over her chest. "Not really." Through no fault of theirs, the picnic with Grant and Abby had felt more like charity than friendship.

She scanned the nearly empty tent. A few minutes

clean-up and she could be tucked inside her cozy house and away from his probing questions. "I got this. Taking down the tent won't be a problem, and there's barely anything left to haul away."

"Not a chance. A good soldier never leaves his battle buddy behind." He flipped one of the tables on its side and began folding up the legs. A smirk crossed his lips when he looked back up at her. "Besides, I want to hear what made you pack up your muscle car and move to Magnolia Springs. I sense mystery in all your evasiveness."

Yeah, like she was going to tell him that story. "Nothing to tell." She grabbed a table of her own. Riley figured her best defense was to deflect his attention. "What was it like in the army?"

Brian propped the table against a nearby fence and turned back to her. "Good mostly." He cupped his chin in thought. "Except for Fort Jackson. Before getting my commission, I enlisted in the Guard and went through basic training between my freshman and sophomore years in college. The noises and smells fifty men can make. And sharing a bathroom..." He shuttered dramatically.

Every time she thought she had a handle on this man, he showed her another facet. She chuckled as much from his antics as the imagery he conjured. "Sounds like the way I grew up."

Riley wanted to bite off her tongue as Brian cocked his head and opened his mouth. Guessing he was about to start a line of questioning she'd rather not answer, she made her own preemptive strike. "Tell me something else about the army. What did you do? Were you a pilot or paratrooper?"

He looked off in the distance for several seconds, giving Riley time to wonder if he'd heard. When he turned his attention back to her, his expression was impassive. "I went to jump school and I used to skydive for sport, but I've been in logistics the past twenty years."

He smiled and the harsh lines of his face evened out. "You know the best thing about the army was the people. Over the years I've worked with some of the best men and women on the planet. No matter how many years go by, I know I can count on them to have my back."

The far-off look in his eyes and the tenderness of his voice showed his words weren't patriotic rhetoric or a recruitment speech. "If being in the army was so great, why'd you leave?"

Brian clenched his jaw as seconds ticked by and Riley's question hung in the air between them. It wasn't like every Tom, Dick, and Bubba in Magnolia Springs didn't know about his injury. What was one more person? The answer was as obvious as the primal need growing inside him. He wanted Riley to see him as a man. To desire him with the same sense of longing that drew him to her.

His attraction went beyond her beauty or fierce loyalty. His gaze swept over her, wanting to soak her up like she was sunshine and he'd been in the dark for years. The couple hours with the two of them working side by side had been the easiest he'd had in a long while. It sucked he couldn't stretch out the moments of being treated like a whole, vital man who also happened to need his ass kicked every few minutes.

Brian resigned himself to the inevitable. She'd find

out sooner or later, and either the facts would alter how she saw him, or they wouldn't. He leaned down to draw the leg of his jeans to the knee, exposing the metal rod of his prosthetic. "I retired from the army when an IED took off both my legs."

Riley's smile dissolved and her eyes grew wide. "Oh God." She cupped a hand to her mouth as tears formed in her eyes. "I've been so horrible to you today. What kind of person am I?"

She paced the small area where they'd been working. "My people skills... Maybe I should stop trying." She spoke more to herself than to him.

He thought for a moment she might bolt from the tent, her anguish and self-effacement evident in the chastisements she continued to murmur.

Instead, drawing in a deep breath, she faced him head on. "Besides being incredibly rude, I've made many assumptions about you which were wrong. I owe you my most sincere apology."

Brian clenched his eyelids. Did his lack of legs excuse his impatient and boorish behavior today? He guessed it did in her book. It also relegated him to the category of people to be dismissed and coddled.

He opened his eyes, ready to tell her what she could do with her apology and pity. Riley extinguished the fiery words poised on his lips. With her head hung, her dark tresses created a shroud around her face.

Brian ached to restore the spark he'd seen today. Reaching through the curtain of her hair, he tilted her chin to meet his gaze. "No worries, sunshine. I'll just expect to see you at next week's Asses Anonymous meeting."

Though a few tears still shimmered in her eyes, the

corners of her mouth turned up. "You shouldn't be trying to make me feel better."

"Then I definitely shouldn't do this." He captured her face with his palms and pulled her in for a kiss.

God! Her lips were soft and tasted like the sweetest strawberries. He meant to release her after a second, but as her lips began to move against his, he gave himself over to the experience. Hunger bordering on starvation drove him on and he licked at the seam of her lips wanting to taste more of her.

Riley opened, letting him plunder her mouth. Her moan as he stroked her tongue gave voice to his own need. Then her hands trailed up his arms to grip his shirt sleeves. The leftover part of his head that wasn't committing every detail to his brain's hard drive, fleetingly wondered if she'd push him away or pull him in for more.

She broke the kiss, slowly extricating herself from his arms. Her breath came in shallow pants as her wide-eyed gaze danced over him. "I'd hate to think what you'd do to me if I really went to pieces."

"Insult me again, and let's find out." Verbal sparring ranked last on his list of things on his mind. Brian pulled her back so she rested in the cradle of his hips and kissed her again.

Desire shrunk their surroundings until the only reality was the feel of his mouth against Riley's. Between one heartbeat and the next, his intentions went from comforting her to soothing his own soul. He kissed down her jaw, craving more of the soft feel of her skin.

Needy noises spilled from her throat, spurring him on. His hand slid from the small of her back to cup her bottom.

"Stop!" Riley shoved at his shoulders, clawing to escape his arms. "If you want to call me a bitch, just do it. Don't tease me like that."

He backed away, his arms raised as confusion washed over him. He thought for a split second the heat had been going both ways.

"I'm sorry. You're right." He'd apologized more today than in the past twenty years and he was getting damned tired of it. Damned tired of screwing up too.

Riley tore out of there without a backwards glance and he let her, watching her disappear into the darkness. He rubbed a hand over his mouth, still feeling the lingering softness of her lips. That kiss had been something else, just like the woman who'd delivered it. There was no denying despite how it had ended. For a man who'd spent a lifetime observing situations, he was making a nasty habit of getting things wrong.

The explosion behind him yanked him from his musing, propelling him straight into hell. The duck-and-cover was pure instinct. His heart pounding in his chest, he scanned the area for a place he and his men could hunker down.

"Over there." He screamed over the continuing sounds of mortar fire. Once he reached cover, he checked to see Wyatt and Howard had followed him. He was alone. "Shit." He darted back.

As he did, his only thought was how had his intel been so wrong. Brian searched the area where his Humvee should have been. Something was off. The terrain around that part of Afghanistan was nothing but rock and dirt. "Wyatt." He fingered the grass that shouldn't be there. Contact with the blades grounded him, bringing him in for a hard landing in reality.

He let out a breath. It had been months since he'd had a flashback. Thank goodness, this one only lasted a few seconds. Brian sucked in several breaths, imagining his safe place. Rarely did he need to use the mind tricks the army psychologist had given to help with the PTSD. He was glad to have them as he still hunkered low to the ground, regaining his equilibrium. Thankfully, the fireworks hadn't triggered the episode until after Riley left. Like she could think any less of him than she already did.

The realization he was back in Magnolia Springs didn't stop the rapid firing of his pulse or the reality of the men he'd lost that day. Brian used his shirt sleeve to wipe the sweat from his eyes. When he agreed to join Maggie and the kids at the park, he hadn't planned to stay for the fireworks. He'd gotten caught up in Riley's eyes and the pleasure of bantering with her and lost track of the time. And forgotten the fact he had about as much business trying to seduce a woman as he had trying to go skydiving again.

God, she took it all away, made him forget everything until he was stupid with need.

He trotted towards his SUV, texting Maggie as he did.

Heading home.

Chapter Four

"You look like hell." Maggie stood at the threshold of Riley's cubical.

Only fitting considering. "Rough night." Twin demons, regret and guilt, tortured her thoughts all night. What was the worse offence, talking to Brian like he was a bully or the guilt at being attracted to a man other than Jake?

It took everything in her to push against what her body screamed for. It had been so long since she'd felt the warmth of a man's touch. The strong arms banding her weren't the ones she most wanted. Her husband had been all lean muscle and not the thick biceps caging her. Still, she felt whole for the first time since Jake's death.

After racing from the park like she was fleeing the scene of a crime, she'd crawled into the shower, staying long after the hot water ran out. Exhaustion wasn't enough to ensure her a peaceful night's sleep. She tossed in her bed, reliving the feel of Brian's kiss and when she finally fell asleep an achingly familiar nightmare paid a call. The first one since moving to Magnolia Springs. The respite weakened her resistance to the terror of replaying her husband's death. Waking drenched in sweat and weeping, she had zero chance of falling back to sleep. She'd hit the sidewalks for a five-mile run she hoped would chase away some of the shadows lurking in the corners of her mind.

"It's the mornings that get me." Maggie pierced her dark thoughts. Her boss/friend pulled up a nearby chair and slumped into the seat, letting her load of purse and laptop bag drop to the floor. "Her Majesty decided the only possible outfit she could wear to school today was one still in the dirty clothes basket."

"No." Glad to be drawn out of her own funk and into the hurly-burly of domestic life, she pushed aside her computer keyboard and turned her attention to Maggie.

She held up a hand. "Wait, it gets better. Matt announced during breakfast he'd volunteered me to bring in six dozen cupcakes for his classes' end-of-the-year party, which is this afternoon."

"What did you do?"

Maggie combed her fingers through her auburn locks. "Thank God, Brian was there. We tag teamed the kids. He threw the outfit in the laundry and volunteered to drive Lexi to school when it was done and I swung by the grocery store.

Riley touched her mouth at the mention of Brian's name. "All that before eight o'clock?" Hopefully, Maggie's drama would keep her thoughts from revisiting last night. It wasn't right for her to take comfort from him. Not only was it wrong considering the way she'd treated him, but he also didn't really mean the heat behind the kisses.

"Yeah, it happens more often than I care to admit. Grocery store cupcakes weren't enough to satisfy Matt. He said all the other moms were making their treats." Maggie shook her head, her lips twisted in a tight bow. "Boy's just going to have to learn his momma isn't

Susie Homemaker."

"Either that or learn how to bake."

Maggie barked a laugh. "I heard that. I'm already up to my eyeballs in alligators here at work without adding pastry chef to my duties." Then she pulled out a thick folder from her laptop case.

Riley took the folder where they'd been keeping all the paperwork on the Victory for Veterans events as Maggie passed it to her. "How'd we do on the concession stand?"

"Two thousand dollars." Maggie beamed.

They were in mid high-five when a masculine voice called out, "Maggie."

"In here, Grant." She stuck her head over the top of the cubical wall.

In a pair of seconds, he stormed up to them. "I might need you to…" He stopped midsentence to give Riley a concerned look. "Are you sick?"

Maggie swatted him on the arm. "You really know how to talk to a lady."

Grant rolled his eyes. "I know." He looked at her. "I'm sorry. I don't mean to be rude but do you need to go home or something?"

She'd seen the dark circles under her eyes. Since she didn't wear makeup she guessed she was doomed to field questions all day. "I'm good."

Grant nodded and turned to Maggie. "As I was saying before I decided to put my foot in my mouth, we won that charter contract between here and Turks and Caicos. You're probably going to have to fly that run until I can hire someone to take it fulltime." He shoved his beefy hands into his pockets and rocked back on his heels. "Abby said to tell you if childcare was a problem she could take the kids for you."

Maggie patted Grant's arm. "The second time was the charm for you."

"Don't I know it."

"Tell her thanks, but between summer camps and Brian, I've got the bases covered. But what am I supposed to do with all the stuff I've got going on here? The golf tournament at Mountain View is in six weeks and I've got tons of details to deal with."

Why hadn't she thought of stepping in sooner? Maybe it was the fog her brain was still in or getting caught up in watching other people's lives. "You know Maggie, I don't mind meeting with Heather tomorrow by myself."

"What and miss spending a couple hours with the Ice Princess?"

"I'll leave you two to settle this one. I'm out of here." With a wave, Grant beat a hasty retreat. Smart man, not to dive into that one with his business partner. Riley learned during her first week of employment, Maggie had no use for Grant's ex-wife. Heather hadn't been that bad. Reserved maybe, but she hadn't seemed to be the devil in a blue dress as Maggie thought.

Her friend had many good attributes, letting go of a grudge, most especially on someone else's behalf, wasn't one of them. Riley made a mental note not to give Maggie reason to lump her into the same category with Heather. "Well, the offer still stands."

Maggie didn't answer right away. Instead she cocked her head, reminding her of the way Brian had sized her up. "You're a good friend." She gathered her purse. "We'll talk tonight when you come to my house for dinner."

Crap! Riley had forgotten about the meeting they'd scheduled. It seemed as if her day was destined to be bookended with troubles.

****

Brian arrived at his section of the street corner, off to the side and back a few feet from the curb where a coven of women waited for the school bus. "Afternoon, Ladies."

Different day, same shit.

Every weekday since last August, they met at this corner and every day the women eyeballed him as if her were some social anomaly. Former high school football star, now legless veteran cares for small children.

The heat seemed especially unforgiving and several of the women fanned themselves and shot impatient looks up the street. He'd been in hotter places and waited for far less pleasant arrivals than screaming children anxious for summer break to begin. As he shifted his weight to keep his back from stiffening, his already bleak mood darkened.

Like every morning, he experienced a few seconds of confusion when he found himself in a soft queen-size bed instead of an army bunk. The weight of remembering followed. Only this time, instead of the reassurance like that of body armor, memories bent his shoulders as if he were carrying a half-ton ruck sack.

Survivor's guilt, the army shrink had told him. Guilt indeed. There were some things in life for which a man should feel guilt. His mind rewound to yesterday and the excitement of being around Riley, especially as she'd shot verbal daggers at him. How could one woman simultaneously make him feel at ease and aggravate the hell out of him? Not that the question mattered. Though it hadn't ended as he wished, it ended the way it should. Why should he be free to live, laugh, and love when the men who'd been on his team could not?

The roar of the school bus's diesel engine yanked him out of his dark thoughts. He plastered a smile on his face and waited for Lexi to tumble off the bus. On cue she bound out of her confinement like a colt let out of its paddock.

"There she is." He ruffled her hair as she twined her arms around his waist. "School's out, school's out. Teacher let the monkeys out." The last thing he wanted was to inflict his darkness on her.

"You're silly, Uncle Brian." She rolled her eyes at him. "School doesn't get out until Friday."

The tightness in his chest loosened at her smile. "Just practicing."

Though he'd never given much thought to having kids, it seemed he'd acquired a pair. It surprised him how natural their routine felt. Once they got inside, he made the same query he did every afternoon. "Got any homework?"

"Nope." She began a dance with her hands clasped in supplication. "Can I go play?"

He bit his lip and dug deep to keep from laughing and telling her 'yes.' Though his dark thoughts were ever present, living with Matt and Lexi made the burden bearable. "After you practice the piano." She dashed off in the direction of Maggie's formal living room. "Don't forget Momma said you were supposed to unload the dishwasher."

Brian spent the next few hours managing the troop of middle school boys who typically paraded through the house once Matt got home. When five o'clock rolled around and he hadn't heard from Maggie, he started dinner.

Learning to cook had been more a function of survival than interest. While most of his repertoire consisted of heat-and-eat, he had a few recipes up his sleeve. As thank you for dealing with his shit yesterday, Brian pulled together the ingredients for his sister's favorite dish. He was tucking the enchiladas into the oven when his sister flew in the backdoor.

"Oh, thank God. You're my new favorite person."

"What's got your hair on fire?"

She rushed past him. "I'll tell you in a second. I gotta change."

By the time Brian set the table, Maggie returned. His eyes widened at her pilot's uniform. She had flown cargo planes in the navy, and now that she'd retired from active duty, she flew twin-engine jets for Davis Air Transport. "What's up with that?"

"The good news is we won the Atlanta to Turks and Caicos route and we've already gotten our first charter." She waved her hand the length of her body. "The bad news is I've got to fly it."

"No worries. I can manage the kids tonight."

She looked at him pleadingly. "Don't hate me."

His spider senses tingled. She'd started too many unpleasant conversations like that when they were kids. "What?"

"I've got to take care of some things on the island so…" She let out a long breath. "I'm going to be gone till Thursday."

Clearly that wasn't the issue. He'd watched the kids for a couple days before. "And?"

"I need you to meet with Heather tomorrow afternoon about the Victory for Veterans golf tournament."

"You know I don't mind taking some of the load off you. God knows, you've got a lot on your plate." It was her junior prom all over again. "But I don't know a thing about the charity or what you're doing with the tournament."

"All you have to do is let Heather show you around the property and make notes where to set up the comfort stations." She held up her hand making an oath. "Promise."

He still wasn't convinced. She was too desperate for that to be all. "What else?"

"Nothing." She shrugged, feigning innocence. "I've got a committee who's up on everything. All you have to do is pass on this. "

Brian took the accordion folder, resigned to the inevitable. "Okay, I'll do it."

Maggie kissed Matt and Lexi who'd come into the kitchen while they'd been talking. "Be good for Uncle Brian and I'll bring you back a surprise."

She stepped into the garage. "One more thing. The committee will be here for dinner in about ten minutes. She's bringing dessert."

There it was, the other shoe.

A few seconds passed. *She?*

He couldn't be that unlucky. The doorbell rang. Yeah, he could. A growing sense of surety built as he moved towards the door. He drew on twenty plus years of practiced military bearing and schooled his expression. It was only a couple hours tonight and a few tomorrow. He could do that. With his hand resting on the doorknob he vowed, no matter how alluring, sassy, or hair-pullingly patronizing she was, he wouldn't let this woman get under his skin.

Brian opened the door. "Hey there." His response started on an uptick before her beauty struck him stupid.

The person he both dreaded and welcomed stood on his sister's porch. Riley had pulled back her dark tresses in a high ponytail exposing golden skin covered by a small tank top. His gaze traveled down the long column of her neck as it eased gracefully into sculpted shoulders.

It's only a couple hours.

"I heard this was where people who suffered from tactlessness could come for support." She flashed a smile before ducking her head.

His jaw grew slack. Her quick wit and shyness obliterated the oaths he'd just made in a one-two punch. It didn't matter that the attraction was one sided or that it would come to nothing. His body craved hers.

Riley hoped a clever opening line would erase any lingering tension from yesterday's string of verbal faux pas. And the kisses they'd shared. However, that wasn't the case. He faltered, his huge body filling the doorway. His heated stare also made an appearance. Would he even let her in the house? "Maggie invited me over."

Riley endured several pounding heartbeats before he responded. "Sorry. Come on in." He stepped back to admit her into a narrow hallway.

Riley peeked around his broad shoulders to the family room beyond. "Maggie and I were supposed to work on the Victory for Veterans golf tournament."

He crossed his arms over his broad chest as he

spoke. "She had to fly that charter to Turks and Caicos and will be gone a couple days. She said to tell you she was sorry she had to leave before she could give you a call."

"Oh, I didn't know. I guess that happened after I left. But that's no big deal." Her voice trailed off as she noticed how the flecks of gold in his eyes made her think of a warm fire on a cold day. Her pulse thrummed and her head swam as he held her gaze. Actually, Maggie's change in plans was a good turn of events, especially if this was how she was going to act when he'd done nothing more than glare at her.

Riley mirrored him, wrapping her arms around her middle, only hers was more from the need to hold herself in check than the display of authority his stance implied. Why was she attracted to a man who so clearly disliked her? She needed to find an escape and quickly, before she added crying to her list of embarrassing things she'd done in front of this man.

At the far end of the family room she spotted the accordion file sitting on the breakfast bar. *Oh, thank God.* Sidestepping him, she crossed the room in strides just short of a sprint. "I'll just take this and be out of your hair."

A girl's sing-song voice stopped her short of her goal. "Hey, Riley."

She bent to greet the girl. "Hey yourself." Lexi's snaggle-tooth grin eased Riley's tension. "How many more days until you're a second grader?"

"Three." She beamed. "What are you doing here? Momma had to go fly one of her planes."

"I heard. I just came by to pick up some stuff from her." Riley palmed the file. "I'll see you again soon."

45

"No." Her bottom lip formed an exaggerated pout. "I want you to stay for dinner."

Riley placed a hand on the girl's shoulder, hoping to ease her way out of the situation with a promise. "Maybe some other time."

"Please."

"How about I leave the ice cream instead?" Riley held up the plastic grocery bag hoping Lexi would see it as a fair trade.

Undeterred, she turned to Brian, who'd played silent witness to the scene. "Uncle Brian, you told me colonels get to tell people what to do. Make her stay."

He cupped her chin. "It doesn't work like that. Riley is a civilian." Then he turned his attention to her, his full lips forming a warm smile. "I could invite her to stay for dinner."

She shook her head, first in confusion then as a refusal. "That's okay. I already ate." Her stomach picked that moment to betray her, rumbling like a freight train.

His lips quirked up and he had the nerve to roll his eyes at her. "You can put your purse in the family room over there." As if that was the final word, he turned towards the kitchen.

Remembering the metal rods of his prosthetics, Riley noted only the slightest hitch in his gate. If she hadn't known, she'd have never guessed he'd lost both his legs. She did however wonder if he had certain limitations, especially when she joined him in the kitchen. The sight of him leaning far into the oven and pulling out an oversized, ceramic baking dish had her envisioning a fall followed by bad burns. "Let me get that for you."

His scowl stopped her midstride. "I don't need your help."

Riley wanted to snatch back her words. "I'm sorry. I didn't mean to infer…" God, why had she let herself get talked into this? "You know, I think I'll take a rain check on dinner."

He let out a breath. "I'm just being touchy. You can get the salad out of the refrigerator. "

Still reeling from the short but intense confrontation, she followed his instructions, placing things on the breakfast room table and filling glasses with iced tea. Soon after, Riley sat at a table to eat for the first time in ages.

Breathing in the spicy scent, she took a bite of enchilada. "This is excellent." The flavor brought back memories of one of the house moms at the children's home. "Do I taste cumin?"

"Yeah. How'd you know?"

"One of my foster moms was from Mexico and that's what she used." Riley flinched inwardly. She hadn't meant to share that.

"One of my buddies was from El Paso. I got the recipe from his mom."

An unexpected feeling of gratitude had Riley's shoulders easing from around her ears. Though she'd been well cared for at the home, the experience of growing up in an institution was difficult to explain to others. Loneliness and an abiding sense of rejection colored an otherwise benign adolescence. She took a deep breath and dove into the delicious food and the sweet sound of Matt and Lexi's laugh, determined not to give her past a seat at the table.

She couldn't, however, prevent a decades old wish

from joining the cozy scene. Towards the end of the meal, when she was sated by an overly full stomach, Riley found herself imagining it was all hers. Her heart clenched with a sense of longing, so much so pin pricks of tears formed in her eyes. She cleared her throat. "Thanks for dinner."

When Riley began stacking the dishes, Brian put his hand on hers. "Don't bother with that." He eyed Matt. "Wild man's got kitchen duty tonight."

Relieved she could soon make an escape, she reached for the accordion folder still resting on the breakfast bar. "I've taken up enough of your evening. I'll just grab this and get out of your hair."

"Here's the thing." His words stopped her where she stood. "Maggie asked me to take over her end of things."

Riley quickly brushed that idea aside. "You don't have to do that. I can handle it."

He met her gaze. "I'm sure you can. I want to help." The unexpected softness in his hazel eyes pleaded rather than commanded.

"All right." She conceded to his request, despite the continued urge to flee. Good sense could overrule strong emotions for only so long. This man brought out more memories, desires, and urges than she was capable of handling. She followed him into the family room and sat when he patted the sofa cushion next to him.

He opened the file and began leafing through the pages. "When I looked through Maggie's notes, I came up with a couple ideas to make things flow a little smoother. I thought we could go over them now, and then I'll meet you at Heather's place tomorrow."

A jolt of adrenaline had her heart pounding. There'd be another day of emotional tug-of-war between them. However, after an hour of listening to his suggestions, she had to admit the guy knew his stuff. Maggie made the right call enlisting her brother's help. "Is this why Grant calls you Brainstorm, because you have great ideas?" The nickname hadn't seemed to fit with his brawn, and she'd wondered at the time if it was a tongue in cheek moniker.

Brian chuckled. "I don't know how great my ideas were when Grant and I were growing up. Sometimes my initials B.S. stand for something else. I remember quite a few times my plans got us either hurt or in trouble. But God, we had fun." His lips turned up in a broad smile that did yummy things to her insides.

All evening, the lid Riley kept on her past had been loosening. Whether it was the way his presence dominated a room or a sense he too had some dark memories of his own, she didn't know. Around Brian, Riley felt safe to remember. "You two sound like Jake and I when we were growing up."

He arched an eyebrow. "Wasn't that your husband's name?"

She clenched her fist as she answered. "It was. Jake and I lived in a church run orphanage. We met the day I was placed there and from that moment on we were inseparable." Her words trailed off as she recalled the years after Jake left the home.

"What happened?"

She shrugged not knowing how to explain it. "He aged out at eighteen. I know he wanted to take me with him, but I was still a ward of the orphanage. I tried to find him once I was on my own but he'd moved so many times I couldn't find him. Years later when we reconnected, things took on a different twist."

Riley had never explained her relationship with Jake and hadn't examined it deeply herself. "I guess coming from similar backgrounds, we felt a connection we didn't with other people."

"How long were you guys together?"

"A little more than five years." Riley closed her eyes as she thought about losing the one person who'd ever wanted her.

"If you don't mind me saying, you look tired."

She dabbed at the corners of her eyes. "Don't worry." She barked a laugh. "I know how bad I look. I've had enough people to tell me already."

"You could never look bad."

Riley's eyes lids sprang open. His voice was so tender.

"You just look tired. That's all." Concern colored his words.

Once again she felt compelled to open to him. "I have nightmares sometimes and once I've had one, I can't go back to sleep."

"I can identify with that problem." He covered her hand with his and sent tendrils of heat up her arm till it warmed her whole body. "The last time I slept more than three hours or didn't wake up in a cold sweat, Bush was in the White House."

The knot in her chest loosened, knowing he wasn't dismissing her problems. In the wake of Jake's death, her few friends had been supportive. However, as the months passed and her grieving intensified, along with the nightmares and fears of death, her friends pulled away. Or maybe Riley pushed them. Growing up knowing she hadn't been wanted, she tended to push people away before they had a chance to reject her.

Riley tugged her hand from underneath his. "I think it's time I was getting home."

His expression hardened before a mask of indifference took its place. "Sure thing."

Riley stood. "Thanks for dinner. It was really good."

Brian nodded and without a word, he headed to the kitchen.

Her emotions raw, she gathered the file in a rush, knowing if she didn't hurry she wouldn't make it to the car before she broke down. Then she had to double back when she realized she didn't have everything.

He met her in the narrow hallway with her purse. "See you tomorrow at Mountain View."

"Ten o'clock."

"Text me, so I know you got home all right."

Riley's head shot up, surprised by the tenderness of his words. "Not necessary. I'll be fine."

His jaw flexed. "Text me."

She nodded and ducked her head, his dark gaze too penetrating to hold. "I will."

Chapter Five

I'm home.

Brian stared at the text for the tenth time since Riley sent it the night before. He'd had to fight the need to hit her up with a rebound text to be sure she'd locked her doors. Thanks to a fuck-ton of personal experience, he was keenly aware of the world's dangers. Human hazards. Mechanical failure. That blind intersection at the crossroad down the way. His mind churned with all kinds of what-if disasters. Hadn't there been two fatalities on that stretch of road last year?

Gloria, the car, crested the hill leading to Mountain View's parking lot. "Thank heavens for that." Trying not to analyze his sudden protective urges too closely, he practically raced to open her door. "Watch the puddles." Heavy thunderstorms moved through the area the night before, leaving muddy potholes dotting the parking lot.

After snagging her things from inside the car, Riley stepped lithely around the puddle. "Thanks." She pushed a pair of sunglasses to the top of her head.

"You look good." Better than good. Delicious. "How'd you sleep?" The image of her silky hair spread out over a pillow flooded his brain. He captured a lock of her hair resting temptingly on her shoulder. Rubbing it between his fingers, he discovered it was every bit as silky as the high gloss suggested.

"I crashed and burned once I got home. And you?" Below a furrowed brow, her lovely violet eyes darted over him then came to rest on the hand that continued to finger her hair. She blushed.

Jeez, when had his hands acquired a mind of their own? He snatched it back and shrugged. "About the same." The dreams he'd had weren't his usual brand of torture. Instead, his imagination had conjured up one sensual scenario after another, all starring her. While the ones featuring Riley were certainly preferable the battle reenactments, they weren't any more restive.

Brian turned his attention to the two-story hotel in the background. "The place looks great." Heather had the structure's roof replaced and the siding repainted.

"Have you been here before?"

"Once." He joined Riley as she stepped onto the concrete pathway leading to the front entrance. "I came with Grant when Heather bought the place last year. The former resort went under when the economy tanked and the owners just locked the doors and walked away."

Brian held the door open for Riley, noting the scaffolding in the foyer. Mountain View wasn't open for business and the Victory for Veterans event would be one of the first since Heather took over. Recalling his previous visit, he led them to the right. "I think Heather's office is this way."

His legs covered the plastic-covered carpet in long strides. Up and amped since the butt crack of dawn, not even two prosthetic legs could slow him down. Except, he needed to stretch the time he spent in Riley's company, not shorten it. Lord only knew how many more times he'd get to enjoy her call him on his bull.

Her gaze took in the new construction, eyes

widening with interest at the architectural details. "Wow, this'll be something when she gets finished. This is even nicer than Belle Jardin."

"What's that?"

"A day spa in Chicago. I worked there for a couple years before I moved to Cincinnati. If things go well with the golf tournament, maybe next year we can ask Heather about adding a getaway package to the fund raiser."

Riley had a lot of history, most of which she wanted to keep hidden. He should respect her privacy, but he couldn't resist pressing for more. "Were you a bookkeeper at Belle Jardin?"

She shook her head. "Davis Air Transport is my first bookkeeping job. I worked as a personal trainer or fitness instructor for about twenty years until I made the career change."

One look at her sculpted arms told him she'd kept up with her fitness routine. "Why'd you change?"

She studied the carpet as they walked down the hall towards Heather's office. "I lost Jake's benefits after he died and I needed a job where I could get insurance. Most places like these don't offer insurance and retirement plans."

Brian understood what it meant to give up a career you loved. "Do you miss it?"

She shrugged then turned to Brian. "Not really. Do you miss the army?"

Every day. While donning the uniform was in the past, he'd spent the last couple months applying to military contractors that might land him a job where he could at least get some purpose in his life. "I miss the challenge, the excitement of never knowing what's around the corner."

Heather Davis stepped from her office, a wide smile on her face. "What do you think of the place?"

Though Maggie continued to bear a grudge on Grant's behalf, Brian couldn't muster the animosity. If his buddy could move on, so could he. "You've come a long way." He meant the statement to cover more than just her resort. She'd changed from fluffy socialite to savvy businesswoman and devoted mom.

"That means a lot." She pointed over her shoulder. "What say we check out the pro shop?"

Riley pulled out her notebook computer from the bag on her shoulder as the three of them walked to the end of the narrow corridor. "If it's all right with you, Heather, I'd like to see the course so we can decide the best places to put the comfort stations."

"No problem." They reached the pro shop and Heather stepped away from them to retrieve a set of keys from a peg board. "You can walk or take one of the golf carts. This one should be charged."

His eyes darted to Riley's athletic body. No doubt she could run the cart path without getting winded. Since quitting physical therapy, he'd told everyone he was now in the fitness protection program.

Riley took the keys from Heather. "Ride or walk?"

Brian appreciated she didn't automatically assume he couldn't walk the length of the golf course, but the truth was he wasn't certain he was up to the task. "I think we better take a cart." He wouldn't let his male pride get in the way of common sense. The only thing more humiliating than admitting to Riley he needed the cart would be if he got to the ninth hole and couldn't get his ass back.

"Okay, but I get to drive." Her mouth formed a mischievous grin.

"Deal."

Note to self, start working out if you want to keep up with Riley.

No amount of exercise could help him keep up with her sharp intellect and sharper wit. Several minutes later, Riley brought the cart to a halt. "What do you think about placing the canopy over there?" She pointed to a stand of pine trees.

He studied the fairway's slope. "I think the volunteers will be dodging golf balls all day." He pointed to the opposite side. "The green cuts to the left, so they'll be out of the way there."

"Good call." She leapt from her seat. "I'm going to check if there's enough level ground between the rough and the woods. Be back in a second." Riley grabbed her tablet and a tape measure then headed across the grass.

Not one to watch while others worked, he climbed out of the cart. "I'm coming with you." He made it two steps. Rain had turned the rough into a swamp. A swamp that had risen over his shoes.

Up ahead, Riley stopped, looked down at her feet, and then over her shoulder at him. "You okay back there?"

"I'm good." She would not babysit him on this project. He motioned her on then attempted a few more cautious steps. His feet squished in the mud, but so far, so good.

Concentrate on balance and weight distribution.

One step at a time. One leg at a time. Just like back in rehab. He gauged the shortest path. Only a few yards and he'd be on steady ground.

The turf had a plan of its own. A plan to remind him pain was never more than a wrong step away. A plan to relieve him of any pride. A plan to rid him of any chance Riley would see him as anything but broken.

Standing still had done nothing to improve his situation. The extra effort it took to pull his foot free of the mire unbalanced him. Overcompensation placed undue pressure on his right leg where his stump fit into the cup at the top of his prosthesis. The metal joint which acted like a knee had some flexibility but not nearly to the extent of a natural joint. Inertia trumped pinwheeling arms and cursing.

He landed on the rough, with a "humph." Another string of muttered expletives followed as he rolled off a jagged rock that cut into his thigh. He cursed the rock, the rain, and the IED that had taken his legs. The sudden intake of Riley's breath had him cursing himself.

Flat of my ass and covered in mud, just the way I want her to see me.

"You all right?" She cocked her head and waited for his response. No cries of shock. No rushing to help. Only patience. The one thing *he* had none of and needed most.

Her calm settled his rage. Not like a thunderstorm extinguishes a forest fire. More in the way a spring rain brought renewal to parched earth.

"I will be." He shifted his weight off his hip and rolled on to his knees. As graceless as that maneuver had been, the next part would be fugly. He chanced a look in Riley's direction. On the other side of the green, she had her back turned to him and was measuring off the area they'd talked about. If he didn't already think she was the best thing he'd met in a long while, that would have done it for him. He worked his way to his feet then retreated to the firmer golf path.

Once he was seated in the cart, he surveyed the damage. The rock had torn a gash in his khakis, which wouldn't have ordinarily been a disaster except it exposed the metal rod of his prosthetic. He always wore pants in public and now she'd ride the whole way back with the evidence of his disability on display.

She climbed into the golf cart and he braced for the mother-hen routine. He fiddled with his pants leg rather than look at her.

Riley bumped his shoulder with hers. "Don't look now, but I think the army gave you a pirate's peg leg instead of one of those cool new prosthetic legs they make now."

His chin jerked up and he caught mischief dancing in her violet eyes as she nibbled on her bottom lit. She was baiting him again, perhaps drawing him into a tirade that would release his pent-up anger. She was playing him like a two-dollar guitar and he loved it.

He leaned over and planted one right on her lips. He hadn't meant to. It was pure impulse to want to wipe that smartass remark off her lips with his own. Given how she'd reacted when he kissed her before, he was probably setting himself up for more of a tongue lashing instead. "That's what you get for making fun of the disabled."

Riley raised a hand to her mouth as a beautiful blush colored her golden skin. "If you're going to do that every time I give you a hard time, I'm going to have to start being nicer to you." She steered the golf cart back onto the path without another word on the matter.

On the other hand, Brian couldn't get his mind off the feel of her full lips. He tried to pull his thoughts to locating the other places they needed to mark for the comfort stations but failed miserably. Keeping his face forward, he chanced a sideways glance. His pulse surged.

Don't read too much into that smile.

****

"That about covers it, boss." Riley handed Grant the stack of June invoices, wishing she could spend a few more days chin deep in spread sheets. Not that she got her thrills from crunching numbers, but the work was a good distraction. "Got something else for me?"

I'll sweep the hangar floor.

Anything to keep her thoughts from playing Monday morning quarterback on her trip to Mountain View.

"What did you do to my brother?"

Riley's head shot to the entrance of her cubicle. Leaning against the opening, Maggie arched an eyebrow and crossed her arms.

Her eyes grew wide. "Excuse me?"

What did he tell her?

Thankfully, Grant chimed in, giving her a moment to regroup. "Did Colonel Grumpy wake up with a better attitude?" He winked at Riley.

Maggie smiled. "Actually, he did."

Riley held her hands up. "I didn't do anything."

Strictly speaking, she hadn't. He'd kissed her. She touched her mouth remembering the hard press of his lips against hers.

Maggie pulled up a chair. "Well, whatever it was, I'm thankful for it. When I left, he was whistling."

"That's the best news I've heard all week." Grant stood from where he'd been resting with his hip cocked on the edge of her desk and patted Riley on the shoulder. "Must have been your doings. I say, you deserve a raise."

Before she spent too much time working out what that kiss meant to her, she needed to know what it had meant to Brian. For those few seconds, she'd known exactly what he wanted from her. Then he'd hit her up with that snarky comment. She'd have bet money his kiss didn't have the same impact it did for her. To him it was probably no more than an extension of their banter. Riley meant what she told him. If she had the occasion to run into him again, she was keeping the conversation strictly polite. No matter how much she enjoyed their teasing or the kisses.

Maggie intruded on her thoughts. "How are we set on the silent auction?"

Riley pushed her issues with Brian aside. She'd already been around in circles trying to sort things out. In the end she decided it didn't matter. Now that Maggie was back, Brian was a momentary blip on her emotional radar. She thought of the nearly two dozen baskets and gift certificates that had been donated. "I'd feel better if we had one or two more."

Maggie nodded. "Me too. I talked to Brian about that and he said he'd hit up some of his buddies from high school for donations."

"Sounds good. How many more should I…" Riley looked at her friend who was eyeing her back like Maggie had something she needed to say but was working out how to word it. "Yes?"

Maggie's eyes softened. "I've really enjoyed working with you on this project. You know that, right?"

Riley nodded as Maggie continued. "Brian wants to see the tournament through to the end." She took Riley by the hand, giving it a firm squeeze. "He hasn't been this into something since before…"

She kept the surprise to herself. Overreacting would only tip Maggie off that something other than event planning went on yesterday. Best to keep that under wraps, considering it would only make things awkward. "No that's fine. He's… fun to work with." When he wasn't screwing with her head.

Her eyes widened. "Really?"

"Yeah, I don't mind." What could she say? I don't want to work with your brother because he made her think about doing things with him that were best left in romance novels.

"No, you think he's fun to be around." Her mouth, which had been open in shock, eased into a smile.

Riley recalled how he'd gripped her elbow in Mountain View's parking lot and eased her past the potholes like they were land minds instead of mud puddles. He'd soaked up every drop of her history she'd shared. And that damn, devilish grin of his that made her stomach do flips. She wouldn't call it fun so much as a form of torture she couldn't get enough of. Taking a few deep breaths, she schooled her features. "Besides even if he wasn't, it's for a good cause."

Tension eased from Maggie's face. "Good." She backed out of Riley's cubicle. "Don't forget we're going shopping Saturday."

The girl's day completely slipped her mind, which showed the effect Brian had on her. She and Maggie decided the dinner following the tournament would have a World War II theme. They'd ordered huge blowups of famous photos taken during the era and gotten a twenty-piece swing band to donate a couple hours so the guests could dance. To cap off the theme, Maggie convinced the volunteers to wear vintage costumes in lieu of formal wear. Maggie, Riley, and a couple other women from the office were meeting at Abby's house in Decatur so they could hit the vintage clothing shops and antique stores that dotted the Atlanta suburb.

Riley moved to Magnolia Springs looking for a place to put down roots. Still, her newfound sense of belonging overwhelmed her. "I'm looking forward to it."

****

Hidden from view behind the dressing room curtain, Riley ran her hand over the vintage dress. The satin fabric caught the light as she turned in front of the three-way mirror. The open back of the dress exposed far more skin than she was comfortable showing.

Maggie called from the other side. "Open up or I'm coming in after you. I endured your comments about that uniform making me look like a prison warden, so it's your turn to face the music."

The girl's day shopping trip was in full swing. After meeting at Abby's, the six-member sorority of volunteers prowled Decatur's eclectic shops for costumes.

Riley rolled her eyes, wishing she'd kept that comment inside her head where it belonged. Taking as good as she gave wasn't nearly as much fun. "Be nice, no more comments about me looking like Ava Gardner."

Tittering laughs bubbled up from the other women. "We make no such promises."

Riley stepped outside the dressing room tugging on the wide shoulder straps of the ivory dress. While it covered her completely from the waist down, the top left her décolletage mostly bare. Time past as Riley's gaze darted to the other women's' faces.

Maggie's face split in a wide smile. "It's a good thing you're my friend, otherwise I'd hate you."

Riley blushed at her friend's idea of a compliment. "I'd don't think it suits me." She brushed her hand over the satin, thinking it would look great on either Maggie's or Abby's curvy figure. "It's too…"

"Flippen hot." Abby finished Riley's sentence with words she never expected to be attributed to her stick figure of a body. "You look amazing."

Riley turned around. "Unzip me. I'm going to just go with the black sheath I tried on earlier."

"The hell you are." Maggie put her hands on Riley's shoulders. "This is perfect and you're buying it."

The sound of her phone going off saved her from having to further argue with her friend. "I better get that." She darted into the dressing room in time to see Brian's number flash on the screen.

"Howdy partner."

Her pulse kicked up a notch at the sound of his voice. "What's up?" To think she had several more weeks of working with him to endure. Her only hope was keeping her snarky comments to herself and to try to not make a fool of herself any further.

"We have a catastrophe brewing. The caterer called to say her assistant double booked them for the day of the tournament dinner and she has to cancel."

"You're not kidding that it's a disaster." It also meant they'd need to spend more time together. "Where are we going to find a replacement at this late date?"

"I thought we could meet for lunch in a little while to do some brain storming."

"Can't." Although as her focus shifted to her discomfort being around Brian to the need to do justice to the cause, she tacked on an explanation. "I rode with Maggie and I need to wait till they're done." She ran through other options, looking for the lease date-like location. "If you give me a couple hours, I can meet you in the hangar."

"I have a better idea." He fired back a response, as if he'd anticipated what she'd say. "I'll pick you up."

She let out a breath. "Fine. We're on Church Street."

"It's a date."

No, it isn't. It's a meeting, and I'll make sure both of us remember that.

When Riley exited the dressing room, Maggie was there to greet her. "For what it's worth, the dress looks lovely on you." Her normally animated face grew serious. "But you should wear whatever makes you comfortable."

"I don't think I have the curves for slinky gowns." She hung the dress on a hook next to a vintage army uniform Maggie intended to buy for Brian.

Mischief danced in Maggie's eyes. "You know what they say. You only regret what you don't buy."

Riley's gaze shifted between the two costumes. If Maggie could convince her brother to wear the uniform, he'd have all the women in the ballroom riveted to his every move. As she eyed the satin dress, she imagined the woman who'd worn the dress nearly eighty years before. It drew her in in a way that made no sense. Brian would never see her as anything other than a fellow volunteer or someone to torture with his jokes. All the same, she couldn't walk away from the gown any more than she could resist the vision of the two of them dressed in the costumes. "Maybe I'll get the salesgirl to hold it for me."

Maggie beamed. "I have another idea as well. Why don't you plan on getting ready in one of the rooms at the resort, and I'll help you with your hair and makeup."

So much for not pushing. A smile tugged at her lips. "I feel like we're in a 70's sitcom where the pretty teen makes over the homely girl." A situation she'd gladly endure for the sense she was finally putting down roots in this small southern community.

Maggie rolled her eyes. "Homely, my round rear end, you are gorgeous."

Riley joined the other women after arranging to pick up the dress later. She tried participating in the conversation while they took turns in the dressing room, only halfheartedly paying attention to their costume choices. Twenty minutes later, when the laughs from the other women died, Riley didn't need to turn around to confirm what her senses were telling her.

"So, this is what you ladies get up to during your hen parties." Brian stood next to Riley. His aftershave brought forth the memory of how his whiskered jaw had scraped against her skin as he kissed her.

Abby winked. "You're in on the secret now."

"It's safe with me." Brian directed his smile at Riley. Did he know what his presence did to her, or was this another example of this teasing?

Maggie stepped from behind the dressing room where she'd been trying on costumes. "What are you doing here?"

He put an arm around Riley's waist, sending her pulse soaring. "I've come to take this lady to lunch."

Maggie quirked an eyebrow. "When did that happen?"

"He called while I was in the dressing room. The caterer is double booked and we've got to find another one."

His fingers tightened on her hip. "I packed my laptop and figured we could find a quiet café somewhere close where we could work."

The contact had her head swimming. Brian joked with every woman he met and they in turn reacted like tweens to a popstar. She was the only one he touched, though. It made no sense. Why her? The inability to understand his actions wasn't a big surprise considering on her best days reading people wasn't a strong suit of hers. And he had the power to spin her around to the point she didn't know which end was up.

His fingers tightened on her hip, moving her along. "Let's head out." He steered her to the front of the store. "Did Maggie talk you into buying a Rosie the Riveter getup?" His gaze locked on hers, a small smile curling the corner of his generous mouth.

Damn, Brian Stone had a way of wielding charm like it was a weapon. Riley bit her lip to keep from laughing. It was an uphill battle. Between his smart-ass sense of humor and his sexy smile, he had a way of getting under her skin that left her dazed and defenseless. "No." She fought the urge to shoot back her own pithy retort.

A warning about the uniform Maggie purchased for him to wear danced at the end of her tongue. Engaging him in banter went against the pledge she'd made to herself. Hopefully, if she managed to act normal for the next hour, she wouldn't end up putting her foot in her mouth or having him put his tongue in it either. He might not mean anything by his method of shutting her up, but it seriously messed with her head.

Her attempted casualness only served as bait for the man who never missed the tiniest detail of what went on around him. He cocked an eyebrow. "That look on your face has me curious." Still smiling, he opened the shop's door for her. "Do I get a preview?"

Just the thoughts of his eyes on her had her pulse racing. She eased past him. "It's nothing special, just a vintage dress."

As they stepped on to the sidewalk, Brian's hand slipped around her waist. It heated her better than the midsummer Georgia sun.

"I'm parked up the street. I know a quiet café close by. It's got free Wi-Fi and the waitresses don't mind if we camp out for a couple hours as long as we keep ordering coffee."

HIs fingers dug into her hip as he propelled them forward. The contact felt possessive, territorial, protective: qualities she told herself she didn't need and was only imagining.

God, to be forty and suffering from my first crush.

Admittedly she wasn't good at reading people, but Brian didn't share her feelings of attraction. He was simply a well-mannered southern gentleman, who had no idea the power his charm wielded or its effect on women.

Brian settled her inside the leather interior, leaning over her to help with her seatbelt. He moved across the front of his car like the warrior he was. Once inside, he turned on the ignition and the latest hit from a popular boy band filled the air.

"Sorry." He switched off the sound system. "It was Lexi's turn to make our listening choices, and as much as I try to be a good influence, the girl seems to have a mind of her own when it comes to music."

"That's fine." She brushed the seat's buttery upholstery. The luxury sedan was by far the most expensive automobile she'd ever seen much less ridden in. Dangerously good looking and good taste in cars, this guy was murder on her resolve.

Minutes later, Brian pulled up to the curb in front of the café. "I've done a lot of my job search from here, so this will be a great place to get some work done." He exited his side and met her by her door as she struggled her way out of the low-slung car. His brow furrowed. "Let me get that for you next time."

"You don't have to do that." Theirs was a working relationship and displays of southern chivalry would only add to the muzzy headed feeling she got around him.

"Humor me." His gaze fixed on hers.

Her cheeks heated, the warmth spreading throughout her body as his hand moved once again to the small of her back. By the time the hostess showed them to a booth, Riley's heart was pounding in her chest.

Within seconds a waitress appeared, her bright smile fixed on Brian. "Hey soldier." She rubbed Brian's back.

Riley tamped down on the roots of jealousy. She had no claim on him and couldn't fault the woman for having good taste.

The waitress turned to Riley. "This guy's something else. Kicked ass over in Afghanistan."

Brian's smile disappeared behind an expressionless mask at the woman's words.

"I'm so proud of him I could bust."

"I appreciate your support, as always, Miss Nancy. When you get a chance, we'd like some coffee and a couple slices of apple pie."

Diving into the pie their waitress brought them as well as the work ahead, they spent an hour making phone calls to already booked caterers, parsing out words on an as needed basis. They finally found one who could meet the price of the original caterer and with that taken care of Brian drove her back to her car with little conversation.

Sitting in Abby's driveway, Riley could no longer ignore his dark mood. "Are you okay?" She ventured into the shallow end of what bothered him.

"Sure, why?"

She shrugged. "You don't seem yourself."

Brian looked away. "I don't like it when folks make a big deal out of my time in the army."

"They're just trying to express their gratitude."

"I get that." His shoulders slumped. "There was no glory in what happened over there and few people who haven't been there understand that. "

Though their pain came from different sources, she had a kindred spirit in Brian. He hid it behind all that southern charm and she simply hid. Riley recognized the expression etched on his face; it had been looking back at her in the mirror for the last three years. She longed to ease some of the pain he hid from everyone else. An idea muscled its way to the front of her brain, one that broke the rule she'd give herself. But it was certain to yank them both from their dark mood.

Oh, before I forget." She stepped out of the car then leaned back in. "Maggie bought you a uniform at Things Remembered. You're going to the dinner dressed as General Patton." She lingered long enough to take in the broad grin on Brian's face before she walked to her car.

Chapter Six

Brian shifted his weight to loosen the stiffness coming from standing for the past twelve hours. Having finally checked in the last foursome, he locked the outside doors of Mountain View's pro shop. With the golf carts juicing in the shed and the loaner clubs back where they belonged, he made his way over to the sales counter and eased onto a high stool. As tired as he was, he wouldn't mind the clock going a little slower. When the day's activities were done, so was his reason for seeing Riley. While he waited for her to tally up the tournament's donations back in Heather's office, he cracked open another water bottle and drained it in one.

Through the glass partition separating the pro shop from the club house, he eyed a group of participants who'd migrated from the course to "The Nineteenth Hole." His girl had totally called it, saying the veterans who were benefiting from the fund raiser should also get to play a round with the celebrities.

A smile crossed his face watching guys he recognized from the sports channel knocking back beers with corporate types, everyday Joes, and men who'd experienced much worse than a ball rolling into a water hazard. Without meaning to, he found himself thinking Wyatt and Howard would have gotten a kick out of meeting one of those guys. Funny, in the past few weeks, replays of the explosion hadn't taken up nearly as much head space as it had before.

The door connecting the pro shop to the main building swung open, drawing Brian's attention from the scene in the bar. Riley breezed in, smiling like she'd won the lottery. That face and her snappy one-liners no doubt played a major role in his frame of mind. She slipped beside him, bumping her shoulder against his. "We rock, you know that don't you?"

Brian wrapped his arm around her waist, stealing a chance to hold her. "Some of us more than others." He covered his affection for her in a joke.

Riley wiggled away, swatting playfully at him. "God, don't hug me. I stink from being outside all day."

She didn't, of course. Instead she smelled of coconut shampoo, freshly mown grass, and something uniquely her.

"What's the tote board say, so far?" He angled the clipboard his way.

Riley ran her finger down a column of figures. "Between the tournament and the tickets from tonight's dinner, the charity's raised Forty-two thousand, five hundred seventy-six dollars." She beamed. "And that's before the silent auction."

"You're amazing, sunshine." She'd poured her heart into making the day a success, planning the event like it was the invasion of Bagdad.

She ducked her head, a gorgeous blush coloring her cheeks. "It was a team effort and we wouldn't have made nearly as much money if you hadn't hit up everybody you've ever known for donations."

A shout from the bar drew their attention. "Looks like a serious game of foosball is going on over there." A quarterback fist-bumped one of the veterans. David

Wyatt, a football fanatic, would have given his left nut to hang out with the eastern division MVP.

When the cheers from next door quieted she leaned in. "Today wasn't too bad for you, was it?" Warmth and concern turned her eyes a deep purple.

He patted his thigh. "No worries. I pre-dosed with some aspirin and the legs have been fine."

She arched an eyebrow. "You might be able to bury other people in BS, but not me."

He let out a breath. The fact she'd call him on his lame attempt at deflection or that she seemed to have a direct line to his thoughts shouldn't have surprised him. Over the past few weeks, she'd shared her struggles to deal with Jake's death.

Their common bond allowed him to open to her just a little. "I'm getting to the point where I can remember the good times I had with my buddies instead of…" He cleared his throat. "Well, you know."

Riley wrapped her hands around his, lacing their fingers. "Yeah, I do."

God, she made everything better. As his chest loosened, he pointed at the soldiers in the bar. "My buddies would have been the first to say those guys definitely earned their moment."

"They have." Then she winked. "You have too. Tonight, we have reason to celebrate." She eased off the stool, pulling away.

He tightened his grip on her fingers a second then released her. Before Riley, he'd never wanted to make a woman his. Hit and run had been SOP for him. Knowing after tonight there'd be no reason for him to see her, left him cold. He'd momentarily considered acting like a normal guy and asking her out, maybe take her to see a movie. Even if he had a clue how to do the relationship thing, Riley wasn't ready. Her heart still belonged to her Jake. So, it was time to let go. "What are you going to do with all your free time now that this shindig is over?"

She shrugged. "Probably nothing."

"No more road races?"

"Not right now. Maybe in the fall. I was thinking about offering some personal training. I've got a gym at home. It's small, but I could probably take on a couple clients." She turned to him. "What about you? Other than video games, got any long-range plans?"

Brian had made it past a round of phone interviews and was scheduled for a couple face-to-face meetings in a few weeks. "I'm up for a couple analyst positions with Mobletech. I'll be heading out to Arizona soon."

"That's awesome." She smiled, her violet eyes sparkling with enthusiasm he wished he felt.

"That makes one of us. I'm not crazy about the prospect of spending the next twenty years chained to a desk. My ass is already flat as it is."

Riley gave him a playful shove. "Your ass is fine. But I know. It's hard being cooped up inside all day."

Even the thoughts of studying intel reports or supervising field agents made him a little squirrelly. "Especially since I've always done things that had a little kick of danger."

Her eyes grew wide. "I just don't get that. Why would anyone deliberately put themselves in harm's way?"

Brian shrugged. "Makes me feel alive. Like I can appreciate everything more when I know I could wake up dead tomorrow."

"Don't say that, not even in jest." Her eyes narrowed.

"I'm sorry, sunshine." He caressed her cheek, hoping to ease the tension he'd caused. "I'm just talking out of my ass. I'm going to take whatever job I can get and be glad of it. Besides who in their right mind would give a legless man a job where he could get the rest of himself damaged?"

Riley rolled her eyes, a small smile playing at her lips. "You're not legless. They just don't go all the way to the ground anymore."

Brian shook his head. "God, I'm going to miss you giving me shit all day."

She palmed her clipboard and turned toward the door, her eyes still sparking with mischief. "I'm going to get cleaned up. I'll meet you in the lobby in a little while, and I promise to give you enough grief to last a lifetime."

****

An hour later, the elevator doors opened with a ding, and Riley stepped into Mountain View's marble lobby. She smoothed her hand over the vintage dress still feeling a little awkward in the overly feminine costume. Scanning the crowd of women dressed in long gowns and men wearing zoot suits, she looked for the resort staff's signature blue and green uniforms. With less than an hour before the ballroom doors would open for dinner and dancing, she needed to go over a few last-minute instructions with them.

First, she needed to speak to Heather. Spying the statuesque woman's head over the crowd, Riley headed to the tables where they'd set up silent auction donations. She worked her way around the rows of tables and waited while Heather finished writing in a bid.

She looked up and a wide smile brightened her face. "You look fantastic." She fingered the sleeve of Riley's dress. "Where'd you get the costume?"

"A vintage shop in Decatur. I wanted to tell you thanks for letting us use your place. This has been really great."

Heather laid her hand on Riley's arm. "You're welcome. I'd like to say I did this solely out of the goodness of my heart." She glanced in Maggie's direction. "But as some people will tell you, I'm not that good of a person. I'm hoping the exposure will be good for business."

Riley shook her head, amazed how her friend could be so accepting of her with all her social awkwardness, but not give Heather the time of day. If the former spouses could be friends, why couldn't Maggie let it go? "You are a good person, Heather and there's nothing wrong with getting a little free advertising."

"I'm glad you think so." She stepped back a few paces and touched one of the auction items. "I see here you're offering a personal training package."

Riley looked at the certificate she'd made. She'd included her picture and a list of services geared towards helping women over forty get fit. "Have I gotten any bids yet?"

Heather's face brightened. "I just upped the ante. You're at two hundred."

"Awesome." With several hours left before they closed the bidding, it looked like she'd meet her goal of three hundred dollars.

Heather arched an eyebrow. "Any chance I could

steal you away from Grant?" Her voice took on a pleading tone. "I really need someone who knows what she's doing. Right now, I've got my appointment girl also doing the admin part of things. She's great and all but a little unorganized." Heather spread her arm to take in the crowded lobby. "You're amazing at this."

Riley had enjoyed the challenge. "That's very flattering, but I think I'll stay where I am."

Heather cocked her head. "It's an open-ended offer."

"I'll keep that in mind."

"I bet you'll be glad when this is over."

Not as much as Riley thought she would. "It's been fun and all, but yeah, I think I'll sleep in in the morning."

She hoped she'd be able to sleep. In the past few weeks, she'd been lucky to get more than a couple hours before she woke startled and breathless. As if that weren't enough, as her attraction to Brian grew, he'd started showing up in her nightmares.

Speak of the devil. The two women looked up as he stepped off the elevator. "I think you're not the only one who's enjoyed this experience."

Her pulse kicked up several notches seeing him dressed in a smart looking black suit. As if her waking attraction wasn't bad enough, her unconscious mind took things to a sensual level. Those were the dreams that had Riley glad this project would be finished in a couple hours. Hopefully, then she could stop dreaming she was making love to him only to have Jake walk into their bedroom to find her in Brian's arms. The sense she'd been unfaithful to her husband ached in her chest.

Brian spotted her, waving his hand in her direction.

Heather laughed as he flashed his devilish grin and he sauntered over. "He's been through a lot, and I'm really glad to see him back to his old self."

Old Brian, new Brian, didn't matter to Riley. Whether he was being Mr. Intimidating or playing the fool just to make her laugh, she couldn't stop from reacting to him. If only spending time with him didn't feel so much like cheating. Just a little longer. Once she wasn't around him so much, her feelings would go away.

When he'd joined them, Heather offered him a hug. "Hey, friend. You and this lady have bowled me away. Everything's turned out perfectly."

"It did, didn't it. It looks like we're going to be able to help a lot of soldiers and their families." Brian's gaze hadn't left Riley's since he'd spotted her across the lobby. Even as he'd been speaking to Heather, he'd been tracking her. Finally, he turned to Heather. "Thanks for letting us use your place. We couldn't have done it without you."

"Sure," She answered distractedly, her attention darting between Riley and Brian.

Damn. All that undercurrent of tension between her and Brian wasn't in her mind. Riley considered for a moment asking Heather if he'd always blown hot and cold like this. Then she remembered after tonight, his mercurial personality wasn't going to be her problem.

The other woman's brow furrowed. "I need to go see…" She pointed aimlessly around the lobby. "Someone… about something." She stepped away but looked back over her shoulder as she retreated. "Don't forget about my offer."

With Heather gone, Brian stepped closer, running

his hand over her shoulder. "You look amazing."

She blushed under the heat of his gaze. "Thanks." Just a little longer and this will be over. She kept her voice light as she answered. "You clean up good. I see you decided not to wear the vintage uniform Maggie found."

He rolled his eyes. "No, I felt like I was an extra in a remake of *Days of Glory*." He brushed his hand over her hair. His devilish grin eased and his eyes darkened. "Let me just say, if the women back then looked as good as you do in that dress, there'd have been a whole lot of GIs going AWOL."

This was one of those times when she didn't know if he was serious or trying to get a rise out of her. She swatted his arm. "You're full of it, but thanks for the compliment." With enough undercurrent between them to drown in, she desperately needed to get away before she did something she'd regret. She took a step back, folding her arms across her body. "They're seating people in the ball room. I better go check things out."

"Sure thing." He stepped aside so she could pass.

Riley headed towards the ballroom. A couple more hours, and she was home free.

He called after her. "I'll catch up to you in a minute."

****

Riley took a moment to take in the scene in front of her. Along the far wall, a band, called Swing Time tuned their instruments. While on the walls to the left and right hung WWII memorabilia Brian got people to loan for the occasion. In the center of the ballroom were dozens of round tables with people milling around finding their seats. It turned out all right, she thought, despite her never having put on any type of party before much less a gala like this. Spying Maggie, Riley headed her way.

"You look great." Both women spoke in unison before breaking out in peals of laughter.

While Maggie had talked her into buying the vintage gown, Riley hadn't let her friend give her the beauty school treatment. Instead, Riley kept her hair simple, pulling it into a tidy twist at her nape before adding just a little color to her lips.

"Everything looks wonderful."

Riley looked around the room. "It was a lot of fun."

Maggie patted her shoulder. "I owe you another thanks. Thanks for being flexible with me handing things over to Brian. It's been a great distraction for him."

"It's been fun getting to know him." With her time with him growing to a close, it seemed okay to give a little air to her feelings about him.

"This has been good for him," Maggie's eyes sparkled with emotion. "*You've* been good for him."

Her friend's words wouldn't sink in. True, they'd grown more comfortable with each other during the weeks working together. That had more to do with her getting better at hiding her attraction to Brian than her doing him any good. If anything, he was probably glad to have other things to fill his time, especially with his job interviews coming up. She hoped he'd find a position that allowed him more than the desk work he hated but also kept him out of harm's way.

"Ladies and gentlemen please take your seats." The MC broke into her worries about his safety.

The two of them followed the instruction, heading towards one of the tables Davis Air Transport reserved. Several of the guys from the hangar and their wives had already taken their seats at one table and spotting an open seat, Riley headed towards it.

"Come sit with us." Maggie pulled out a chair at an adjoining table. As Riley took her seat, Maggie made the introductions. "This old married couple is either Abby's son and daughter-in-law or Grant's sister and brother-in-law, depending on how you want to look at things."

"Pleased to meet you." Riley processed the convoluted introduction. Her boss and his new wife were related by more than their own marriage.

Her attention shifted to the guy across from her. "I'm Chris Mueller." He held out his hand for her to shake. "I'm a friend of Abby's."

He was nice looking, although she was biased towards men with rugged features while Chris was cute enough to grace the covers of magazines. He also had a mischievous grin that suggested he'd keep the table entertained if given half a chance. Riley returned his smile, offering her own introduction.

As she tucked her napkin in her lap, a warm hand trail across her back. The caress sent licks of electric energy along her skin. No need to look behind her when her body was tuned to the Brian Stone frequency.

"Evening, everyone." His gaze lingered on her, as he took the seat to her left.

Though they'd spent countless hours together in the past few weeks, when he looked at her like that her brain shorted out. She drew in a breath, hoping her reaction to him went unnoticed.

"Relax." Brian leaned in so only she could hear. "We've done everything we can, so it's time to enjoy our evening."

Riley tried to give the outward signs she'd taken Brian's suggestion. Too bad she couldn't control her heart and stomach the way she could her shoulders. Thankfully, the dinner hour moved seamlessly. The last-minute caterer she and Brian found surpassed her expectations.

As the evening progressed, it was his turn to tense. As dessert was served, Grant left the table and walked to the front of the room. Brian's back stiffened as it had done the day they'd gone to the coffee shop.

"You'll be fine. Picture everyone in their underwear."

His gaze darkened. "Not going to help, I'm afraid."

"Maybe not." She ducked her head reminding herself she had only a couple hours more to wonder the meaning behind his stares. Strangely, the thought didn't cheer her the way it should.

Grant took the podium, drawing their attention forward. "Before I turn the program over to our speaker, I'd like to take this opportunity to thank a few of the people who helped make this night possible. First, Heather Davis for donating the use of Mountain View, all the guys who volunteered for the golf tournament, vendors and individuals who donated to our silent auction, our first fund raiser wouldn't have been a success without your help." Then Grant raised his arm pointing to the back of the room. "I'd also like to thank Riley Logan and Brian Stone for donating their organizational skills."

Thankfully, Riley's time in the spotlight was short

lived, but that didn't mean Brian was off the hook.

B*etter him than me.*

Grant's smile broadened. "Now, I'd like to introduce a man many of you know. Following his graduation from Magnolia Springs High, Lieutenant Colonel Brian Stone attended the University of Georgia where he received a degree in engineering. He went on to serve in the army for twenty years, during which he spent eight of those years in Iraq and Afghanistan. After recovering from his injuries, he returned to his hometown where he has helped to raise his niece and nephew as well as volunteer for Victory for Veterans. I'm please to call the guy my best friend."

Riley leaned in. "You've earned this recognition."

"It feels more like punishment than reward." Brian stood, jerking his jacket straight and raising his chin.

As he walked towards the podium her heart thudded, partly in empathy but also because he captivated her attention. She could easily see why men had followed him into danger. Brian mounted the dais like he did everything else, with cocky confidence. Confidence he could back up with action.

"When I was laying in the hospital bed in Germany, all I could think about was coming home. I had a laundry list of things I wanted to do, beginning with hugging my niece and nephew and ending with sharing a cold one with this guy." He pointed to Grant.

"But coming home wasn't easy." Brian paused, emotion playing across his face.

Riley's own heart responded, knowing it wasn't public speaking behind the silence, but the memory of what it felt like to stare in the face of change you didn't want. Riley held her breath, exhaling only as he started again.

"The army has a term for that moment when they turn you loose on your family: reentry." Brian paused again, looking up as if contemplating. He nodded. "Sounds about right, considering like a meteor, some of us burn up upon reentry. Sure, the army has programs, but that doesn't take care of transportation to the hospital, housing, or finding a job when being a soldier is they only thing you know how to do. Or the emotional issues that arise from experiencing things you hope to God no one you love ever does. Victory for Veterans fills in those holes." Brian scanned the audience, holding them all in his gaze. "On behalf of the soldiers seated out there and the dozens in the community you've helped, thank you."

Amid thunderous applause, Brian returned to his seat, several guests stopping him along the way. Riley met him as he returned to the table, pressing an impulsive kiss on his cheek.

His eyes widened, but before she had a chance to regret letting her mouth get the better of her again, he rolled his eyes at her. "Jeez, it wasn't the Gettysburg address, for crap's sake."

She chuckled. "It was still very well done. Give yourself some credit."

Before she could say any more, the band struck up *Chattanooga Choo-Choo* and within seconds the two married couples left the table. Brian left the table as well, offering the excuse of needing to make a phone call. She considered going after him, but figured he wanted some time to himself. No doubt, he hadn't intended to reveal quite so much in his speech.

Riley nodded, letting the dancers draw her

attention and her ears perked up when Chris leaned over to Maggie. "My usual partner is occupied. Would you like to dance?"

She shook her head. "The only dance I know is the Electric Slide and if memory serves me correctly, that didn't gain popularity until sometime later." Her gaze darted across the table. "But I bet Riley would like to."

She liked dancing even if she didn't do it particularly well. It'd been something she and Jake had enjoyed.

Chris held out his hand. "How about it?"

These people had pulled her out of herself to the point where she didn't need to think about her response. "I'd love to."

****

"How you doing?" Grant sidled up to Brian as he stood at the back of the ballroom.

He'd returned to find in the five minutes he'd been gone, Riley had been swooped up by some GQ model dressed in a goddamned zoot suit. "Fine." Though he felt a long way from fine.

Grant barked a laugh. "Then why do you look like someone kicked your dog?"

Brian stiffened. "Don't know what you're talking about." Tension coiled in Brian's belly like a rattlesnake.

"All right, if that's how you want to play it."

His gaze locked onto Riley without needing to search the room. It was as if he had some inner compass and she was his true north. As Abby's friend twirled them around, light reflected in warm shimmers off Riley's body. He wished it were he who had the privilege holding her, or at the very least that she were standing at the back of the room with him as he fought against the twin demons of memory and regret. If she was, she wouldn't have taken that off of him. She'd have shoved his attitude right back at him then glared at him until he spilled.

Brian wanted to talk to Grant, maybe get some pointers since he'd managed to land a great lady. His eyes shot back to Riley as she danced. She could do so much better than him.

"For heaven's sake, go ask her to dance."

"What?" Had his friend lost his mind?

Grant flashed a grin. "I've seen the way you look at her. Go over there and cut in."

Brian shook his head. "She's spent enough time with me lately that she's probably dying to get rid of me." He really wanted to hip check Abby's friend and take the gorgeous woman in his arms.

Grant cocked his head, studying the couple dancing a few feet in front of them. "I wouldn't bet on it."

When she wasn't calling him on his shit, Riley remained politely distant. Nothing about their interactions gave any indication she saw him as anything other than a fellow volunteer. Despite gifting him with a kiss moments before. "I seriously doubt that." She was simply showing the sweet side to her personality everyone kept claiming she had.

Grant elbowed him. "What, you're not up for a challenge? Your problem is you've never had to work to get a woman." He nodded towards Riley. "I'm telling you. This one's not going to throw herself at you like the others have. Dance with her. Ask her out. Don't let her get away."

"She's got some stuff she's going through. I don't

think she's ready to start anything." Besides the dark places between his ears, there was also his total lack of experience in the normal dating process to consider.

Thankfully, Abby came up to them, stopping him from having to offer up more lame excuses. "Come on, let's dance." She tugged Grant's hand.

The reluctant Fred Astaire groaned and pretended to drag his heels. "I already got you woman. I thought I wasn't going to have to do this anymore."

Abby laughed. "Silly man. I want to reenact our first dance."

Grant looked over his shoulder as he moved towards the dance floor. "I'm telling you, man. Find a way to make it happen. The good ones are worth the work."

Brian shot another look towards Riley and Chris before heading out to the lobby. What he needed to focus on was the interviews coming up in the next few weeks. Somehow, the thoughts of scoring a job that chained him to a desk for the next twenty year didn't stir much of a reaction. Not like one where he could at least be in the field occasionally, or the way spending hours with Riley did. Too bad there wasn't a way to do both.

One of the silent auction donations caught his attention. He stepped closer, a plan forming in his head. They didn't call him Brainstorm for nothing. If he could pass the physical requirements, perhaps he wouldn't have to be a desk jockey after all.

Chapter Seven

As Chris escorted Riley back to their table, she didn't know what hurt more, her feet from trying to keep up with him, or her sides from laughing at his jokes. "That was a lot of fun, thank you." She collapsed into her chair.

"The pleasure was all mine." He kissed her hand.

"You southern men certainly deserve your reputation."

For someone who was more comfortable with her own company than that of others, Riley had enjoyed this evening more than she thought possible. As she caught her breath guilt pricked her. "Where did Brian go?" She shouldn't be off having fun while he was working.

Maggie looked over her shoulder to the back of the ballroom. "He was skulking over there earlier, but I don't see him now."

"I should probably find him. There might be a problem back in the kitchen." Or worse, he'd slipped into the black hole of memories.

As she stood, he eased behind her. He seemed to have beaten back whatever dark thoughts that plagued him after his speech. As he sat down, his hazel eyes snapped, making her think he was up to something. "Where'd you go?"

He flashed a smile. "Checking out the baskets in

the lobby."

She wasn't buying the innocent act for a second, but as Grant took the podium again, she left that thought for another time. The silent auction was her baby and she crossed her fingers that it would bring in enough to fund a job fair she wanted to have.

As the winning bids were announced, Riley's emotions swirled inside her. The attendees were generous, which filled her heart with gratefulness and her mind with plans for how to help the veterans. She was also sad her time working with so many great people was ending. Especially one in particular.

Riley cut her eyes to Brian. The scar running the length of his jaw called to mind this dark past. While the way he filled out the shoulders of his suit jacket reminded her of his strength, both inside and out. And his sensual lips… she didn't need them to remind her of the kisses they shared.

She let out a breath. For all that she would miss Brian, it was for the best that their time working together was ending. Maybe now he'd stop consuming her thoughts and playing the starring role in her dreams.

The sound of her name being spoken over the sound system pulled her into the present.

See, even now he consumes my thoughts far more than is sensible.

"The final bid for Riley Logan's donation of eight weeks personal training raised…" The excitement in Grant's voice grew. "One thousand dollars."

"Holy cow. Who in the world would have bid that?"

Grant answered her question. "The bid is awarded to Brian Stone."

His grin just kept widening. "You just thought after tonight you were rid of me."

Her jaw dropped.

That's not right and he damn well knows it.

She'd meant that for women only. If he thought he was going to get away with his stunt, he hadn't learned much about her in the past few weeks. "Why did you do that?"

He shrugged as if he hadn't just made her life much harder. "I need to get into shape."

Riley clenched her fists. "I meant to offer this to another woman."

"Contact a couple of the ladies who lost out, see if they're still interested."

Didn't he just have all the answers. He wasn't addressing what should have been his top concern. "I don't have any expertise in helping people with…"

He arched an eyebrow. "Amputations. It's okay to say it."

His words heated her cheeks. That wasn't the real reason why she didn't want to help him, but she could hardly explain her attraction to him.

He didn't seem to notice how flustered he'd made her. "It doesn't matter. What I need is someone to kick my ass when I get lazy and since you've been doing that for the past several weeks, it should be old hat to you."

"Why me? Why now?" It wasn't fair to expect her to continue resisting him or enduring the torture of watching his hard body in action as he trained.

"I've decided to interview for a field agent position with Mobletech."

His good news brought her anger down to jalapeno

levels instead of Habanero. It still didn't make sense. "That's great, but what does that have to do with me?"

"I have to pass a PT test in order to take the job."

Riley recalled the few details he'd shared about his job in the army. He'd been oblique because most of it had been classified. What he had shared scared the shit out of her. She broke out in a cold sweat. "I won't do it." She took a step back, shaking her head. "You'll have to find someone else."

He took her hands. "It'll be fun. I promise not to be a pain."

His pleading did nothing to her resolve. Brian Stone could beg, promise, and cajole and she wouldn't budge. "I'm not going to help you do something that could get you killed." Never again would she put herself through that. Her sanity wouldn't hold up if she lost another man to something preventable.

"Is that all, sunshine?" He cupped her cheek in a way that tested her resolve. "The closest thing to danger I'll come to is watching a caravan of trucks move through a field."

"You swear?" She clung to the promise. Regardless of whether he was in her life, she couldn't stand the thoughts of what his death would do to Maggie and her kids.

"Scout's honor." He raised his hand. "This job is a step towards me getting back a part of my life."

"Couldn't you just join a gym?"

"I could. In fact, I've gone a couple times. It felt like everyone there was waiting for me to fall. The trainer hovered worse than Maggie. I'd like to take my licks out of the public eye."

"I can understand that." She sought his eyes,

searching for a pledge. "And your new job isn't going to send you back to some dangerous country."

"The closest thing I'll get to a hot spot is looking at pictures. Since you're committed to helping soldiers, you can look at it as your patriotic duty, if you like."

"Manipulate much?" The last of her resistance gave way.

"Every chance I get."

Wasn't that the God's honest truth?

She was in so much trouble and couldn't do a damned thing about it. "All right, we'll start Monday after work." She could give him a warning though. Riley raised a finger. "Come prepared to sweat."

****

Riley watched Abby as she worked to lift the two-pound hand weights. She'd followed Brian's suggestion and contacted the top three bidders from the silent auction to see if they were interested in having a personal trainer. "One more rep and you're done."

Abby grimaced as she lowered the weight. "I think I'm done now."

"What happened to you wanting nicely sculpted arms?" Riley had her clients set goals when they worked with her. It helped to know what they wanted so they could stay motivated.

"You're killing me." Abby huffed a couple breaths but didn't give up.

"Eight more. I promise you can do it. Think how good you'll look in that bathing suit you bought last week."

Perspiration trickled down Abby's face.

"That's enough." She took the weights and placed them on the rack. "That was a good first session."

The other woman shook out her arms. "How am I going to get my clothes off when I get home?"

"I think you'll find someone to help you with that."

Abby turned to look in the mirror. "God, I'd scare little children."

Riley passed her a towel. "If your make up still looks good after a workout, you weren't doing it right." She laughed. "You really did work hard, though. Make Grant run you a warm bath when you get home and I'll see you Wednesday."

Abby followed Riley as she led the way back through her home. "I love seeing this house again. Really takes me back to my childhood." She'd shared on her first session that she grew up down the street and one of her childhood friends lived in this house.

Riley looked around at the blank walls. "I keep meaning to paint or hang some pictures, but I never seem to get around to it."

"I like the minimalist approach." Abby tapped her finger to her lips. "Gives the place an open feel."

Bare more like it.

"I sold most everything when I moved down here. I wanted to make a fresh start and the stuff had too many memories."

"Other than Gloria."

Riley echoed the woman's smile. Some things were too precious to lose. "Couldn't let her go." She motioned around the open space of her combination living/dining room. "All this was supposed to help me move on." Riley's voice trailed off as she realized she hadn't moved on, only moved. So much of her head space was spent reliving her past.

"You'll get there when you're ready." Abby patted

her hand. "I've never lost someone the way you have, so I can't say I know how it feels, but I do know what it's like to feel like you're spinning your wheels. "

"That's kind of you to say."

"That's what friends are for. I'll see you Wednesday." Abby grimaced as she waved. "If I live that long."

Riley turned to survey her tiny living room. Maybe a nice yellow would look good on the walls, something cheerful but not too bright. Her landlord said he'd reimburse her for the supplies if she wanted to paint. It wouldn't take too much work. The biggest chore would be emptying the three bookshelves lining the length of one wall.

She planned what she needed to buy till the doorbell got her feet moving. Her pulse thrummed as she made her way to her front door. A potent cocktail of dread, desire and anger swirled in her system, making her head foggy. She blew out her breath in a harsh rush.

Brian had the nerve to Shanghai her donation and then guilt her into agreeing to train him. Though, if she was honest with herself, she already missed the phone calls, texts and emails they'd exchanged leading up to the tournament.

Pitiful, considering it's only been a few days since I've heard from him.

She jerked open the door, determined not to show Colonel Bossy how much he got under her skin. One look at his dark gaze and she forgot her promise. Forgot to breathe. Forgot her own name.

"Hello there, sunshine." Dressed in a tight-fitting T-shirt, he looked habanero hot. When she didn't answer, he added. "I wasn't sure which door to use."

Riley drew in a steadying breath. "This one's fine." Her voice quivered. Considering how much time they spent together while planning the Victory for Veterans event, she should have grown accustomed to being around him. She couldn't chalk it up to the time away. Even when they'd been in daily contact, he affected her this way. Having him in her home only added to the tension.

Her gaze drifted to the flowers clutched in his fist. He thrust them towards her. "Maggie suggested I start off with an apology for being a pushy bastard, and the kids suggested I bring a little good will gift."

His impish grin didn't match his normally harsh expression, but she loved it all the same. "Sorry I'm mad at you or sorry you did it?"

"Sorry you're mad, definitely."

Riley rolled her eyes. "At least you're an honest pushy bastard."

He invaded her space. "Although I don't understand why you're mad, I thought we worked well together."

Her pulse reacted to his nearness. "I guess I overreacted, especially in light of your explanation." She put some space between them, thinking if she didn't he would hear her heart pounding.

"Am I forgiven?" Brian's hand brushed over hers during the exchange.

Was it her imagination, or did his fingers linger in the passing? "Of course. The flowers are nice. Let me get a glass for these." When was the last time she'd received flowers? Jake hadn't been the romantic type, so the last time had been…never.

She lingered in the kitchen. "Are you ready to get

started? My gym is this way."

He surveyed the enclosed garage. "Wow, I'm impressed. This is a great set up."

Riley looked over her collection of used equipment. "Thanks. I got most of it at Second-hand Lions over on Piedmont Street."

Brian moved to examine the weight machine. "This is top of the line."

Thank God for safe topics. "People make resolutions and buy stuff that sits in their garage or bedroom." She reached for the form she'd made up. "I know you said you just wanted a private place to do your workouts, but I thought it would be a good idea since I am a certified trainer if I got some personal stats on you. Just to be sure you're in good health."

"No problem. Don't want to drop dead on you."

Riley flinched.

"Sorry. That was crass." He took her hand.

Riley pulled away. "Let me take your blood pressure." Better to forge ahead than explain her automatic reflex.

"I guess that covers everything you didn't already know." He passed her the clipboard. "I have several pieces of shrapnel lodged in my lower back, and a couple dozen scars." He held up his left hand. "Oh, and I don't have much strength after they sewed my ring finger back on."

"Other than that, you're in perfect health." Riley marveled he'd survived the explosion. She tried not to compare Brian's accident to the one that claimed Jake's life. Both had been doing a dangerous job for all the right reasons. At least God had been merciful to someone. "Let's get started."

"You're the boss." He followed close on her heels.

"Don't you forget it, or I'll have you drop and give me twenty."

He flashed one of his trademark grins. "I just bet you would. By the way, that's also part of the PT test. I have to do pushups and sit-ups."

Riley slipped into trainer mode. "After a warmup, that sounds like a good place to start."

Through force of will she managed to keep herself clinically distant while Brian began his workout. Though he claimed to have been completely inactive since returning home, he still moved with practiced ease. "I'm impressed. You're almost where you need to be."

He rose from the mat, moving more fluidly than he had when they first met. "They worked on my upper body in rehab and I've kept that up." He eyed the pair of treadmills. "My cardio sucks though. I got new prosthetics a while back. These fit better."

Instead of looking to his lower extremities, her eyes stayed on the broad muscles of his chest. Riley had trained hundreds of men over the past twenty years, some of whom were professional athletes. None of those bodies got to her the way Brian's did.

After running on the treadmill, he shifted to the weight bench where the sight of his muscles moving fluidly fed her already hungry lust. Her body reacted to his in a way only one other man had been able to call forth. Heat radiated off his sweat soaked skin, making her wonder how it would feel to absorb the warmth into her own.

She swallowed hard. "I think you're good. Don't want to push too much."

"I've still got a little juice in me." He set the bar on the rack and grinned. "That felt good."

He looked good doing it. "Here, you need to hydrate." She handed him a water bottle.

He drained it in one long draw, sighing at the end. "I'm going to sleep like a baby tonight.

"Good." That wouldn't be the case for her. She could look forward to hours of watching his deltoids bunching in her dreams.

"I have an idea." He tugged her down to the bench.

She tensed. Problem was so did she, a very naughty one that involved him making love to her. "What's that?" Heat bloomed in her belly.

"Tomorrow why don't you work out as well? You've got two treadmills and I could spot you on the weights." Brian brushed back a tendril of hair.

Riley shivered at the contact. Thankfully, he seemed oblivious to the effect he had on her.

"We could make it a friendly competition."

She leaned in, unable to resist tasting his lips. "Sounds good." Longing won the battle with good sense. Guilt would torture her dreams, but she could no more stop herself than she could turn back time. When his mouth began moving with hers, she changed her mind. She'd gladly trade hours of hell for a few seconds of heaven.

Brian deepened the kiss, pulling her into his body as his tongue plunged into her mouth. He devoured her with a thinly veiled hunger.

Her hands raked through the short strands, loving the rough feel of his brush cut against her fingers.

He pulled back, only to trail kisses across her jaw and down her neck. They could hardly be called kisses though. They were more like tiny bites he soothed with his tongue. He tugged at the strap of her tank top, pulling it and her sports bra down her shoulder. He pushed her clothes further, exposing her breast that he cupped with his hand. "I knew they'd be beautiful."

She was small which worked well with the amount of jogging she'd done. But she'd never liked that they made her feel less than womanly. His kisses turned gentle as his mouth followed where his hands had been.

Riley inched forward. "Make love to me."

Brian's head shot up. His face twisted, first in anguish then anger. "I can't." He bolted from the seat.

Heat flooded Riley's cheeks. Her fingers shook as she covered her exposed flesh. "I'm sorry." She longed to wind her arms around him, pulling him in. Everything about his body language screamed, "Leave me alone."

"You have nothing to be sorry for." He cut the air with a swipe of his hand. "This whole thing was a mistake."

Guilt tore at her. He'd come to her for a place where he wasn't constantly reminded of his injuries and she'd betrayed that trust in the first hour. "Please, don't go. I don't understand what came over me."

He turned to face her, his eyes darkening until they were nearly black. "I know what came over you. You expected me to be a normal guy. But I'm not normal. Far from it."

"I'm not exactly the poster girl for good mental health." She despised herself in this moment. "Or professional. It won't happen again." She followed him to the door.

"You can bet it won't. I'll find some other way to

get up to speed." With that he strode to his car, leaving her feeling like both an idiot and a failure.

Chapter Eight

Late the next day the inevitable happened. Maggie stopped by Riley's cubicle. "How'd it go with Brian last night?"

She didn't look up from her computer. "Fine."

Her friend popped her hip against the desk. "That is exactly what he said."

Several seconds passed before she could muster the will to look up, and when she did, she immediately regretted exposing herself to Maggie's penetrating gaze.

"Funny, neither one of you look fine."

How did she look? How did heart ache manifest in her body? How did causing humiliation read on her face? It had never dawned on her his injuries affected his ability to become aroused. But he had been, same as her. She'd seen it in his eyes and felt it in the way he touched her. He couldn't take their attraction to its logical conclusion. Make that *primal* conclusion; there was nothing logical about what they'd done. He simply couldn't make love to her.

Going for her best fake-it-until-you-make-it routine, Riley changed the subject. "I was going to leave right at five o'clock unless you have anything important you needed from me."

"Is Brian coming over to work out again?"

Not hardly.

"I'm painting the dining room and I wanted to get the first coat on before bedtime."

Maggie eyed Riley again. "Let me know if you want some help."

The second the clock on her computer hit five, Riley grabbed her purse. An hour later she was lugging paint cans inside, setting them on the hardwood floor in her dining room. After spreading the drop cloths, she studied her supplies. The place she'd shared with Jake had been a new condo that hadn't needed a thing when they moved in. She couldn't recall the other places she'd called home. They'd simply been stopping points along the way to nowhere.

"How hard could this be?"

As Riley fell into a rhythm, her mind played over the night before. In a roundabout way by running him off, she'd solved her problem. At lease now she wouldn't have to worry about hiding her attraction.

She'd gotten one wall done and another about halfway when the doorbell sounded. After laying the roller back in the tray, she glanced at her reflection in the mirror. Yellow dots of paint freckled her face. She was in no shape to answer the door if she cared what she looked like. Which she didn't. It was just as well considering the person on the other side hammered the door again. "Hold your horses." She looked through the peephole. "Good Lord, why are you here?"

"To work out."

Riley opened the door to Brian, wondering what changed his mind. Her gaze immediately shifted south. He wore a pair of nylon workout shorts. Stopping at the knee, they put the metal rods of his prosthetics on full display.

Anger flamed inside her. "I thought you didn't want my help."

He shrugged as he moved passed her. "Funny, I don't remember saying that."

If he could pretend last night never happened then so could she, though it hurt that he felt she needed a reminder of what the IED had done. "My mistake. Give me a couple minutes, I'll get changed." She pointed towards her work out room. "Why don't you go on through and get started. You can begin with the hand weights."

After changing into workout gear, she paused at the threshold to her makeshift gym. His biceps bulged with each curl. She banked the physical reaction the view caused. Mastered her emotions. She'd trained dozens of men just as cut as him. "How many is that?"

"Five reps of eight."

None of those guys had the power to draw her in. "That's enough. Move to the bench."

The heat in his gaze sucked the breath from her lungs. Why did he do that to her?

They worked in tension laced silence, him lifting and her spotting. It wasn't until he'd worked his way up to two hundred, twenty-five pounds, that he needed her assistance. Gripping his wrists, Riley supported him as he hefted the barbell back in place.

"You're up." He shifted off the weight bench.

Riley took her turn, mostly succeeding in pushing his presence from her mind as she worked her upper body. Then as she lifted the weight back to its place, she had to swallow her surprise. He was fully aroused. Their eyes locked for a second before he looked away.

Confusion washed over her. He'd said he couldn't,

which she took literally. Realization dawned on her. *Oh, it was like that.* Her cheeks heated. She was such a fool. It wasn't that he couldn't. It wasn't what he wanted. His reaction now was simply a function of biology.

Riley bolted from the bench, anger flooding her system and twisting her stomach. Why had he lied? She was a big girl and could take the truth.

"Are you done?" His question rolled like gravel across her emotions.

"Very." She turned her back, busying herself with the sudden need to rearrange the stack of towels. "Just give me a second and I'll spot you."

"No hurry."

She fought the urge to storm out, but this was her place and she wouldn't let his rejection send her running. But God, she didn't want him to see her upset. She thumbed away her angry tears. It was all too much. "Could you give me a second?" She escaped into her kitchen. "I need to refill this bottle."

The sound of his steps echoed hers. Yeah, he couldn't even give her that much. He caught up to her in the kitchen, cornering her between the table and the counter.

"I'm sorry, sunshine."

Riley pushed at his shoulders, for all the good it did her. He didn't budge an inch. "Damn you and your apologies." Why couldn't he spare her further humiliation?

He brushed her tears. "I'm sorry I made you think I had more to give."

What did that even mean? Was she asking for more than she should expect from a man? "Just go, okay."

"Not until I make you understand." He kissed her tears, pressing his lips to both cheeks. "Physically I can make love but…"

Jesus, I don't need you to spell it out. "I'm not stupid. You don't want me."

He drew her hand to the front of his shorts. "Oh, but I do want you. Very much. I just don't think it's a good idea."

It wasn't and she knew it, but sometimes a bad idea sounded so damn good.

Brian hated himself for letting Riley think for one second she wasn't the most desirable woman he'd ever met. One thing held him from showing her how much he wanted her. His legs. Or lack thereof, as the case was. How would it work, making love to her?

The look on her face helped him beat back that concern. This wasn't about him. Through his stupidity he'd caused her to think he didn't want her more than he wanted his heart to keep beating. It was his job to rectify that misconception, and he was a man who took his assignments seriously.

Maybe he couldn't make love to Riley in the way most couples did, but that didn't leave him without options. "Let me make you feel good." He trailed kisses across her jaw.

"Oh, God." She leaned into him.

Her feminine sigh sent shock waves straight through him. "That's it, baby. Give yourself to me." He kissed an especially sweet spot behind her ear. Then he worked his mouth down the slender column of her neck.

Riley grabbed onto him, her fingers digging into his back. He couldn't take the anticipation another moment and backed them towards her bedroom. His hands caressed the soft skin of her shoulders. When they reached her room, he stripped the shirt from her body, but her snug fitting sports bra stood in his way. He went to work on it, drawing it over her head. It might not have been the most elegant undressing, but the view was well worth the struggle.

She was a woman who should never wear clothes. Her golden skin was perfect, glistening just the least bit from the sweat of their exertion. "Let me touch you."

Brian immediately complied, eager to give her anything she wanted. He stripped off his shirt and lay next to her.

"I've wanted to do this since I met you." She traced the outline of his muscles. "There's such power beneath your skin. It entrances me."

"It's you with all the power. You have me at your mercy, and I could spend hours on your lips alone. To say nothing of the other things I'd like to discover."

He'd never had a committed relationship with a woman, just a series of short-term hook ups that left him feeling cold. For a split second he was jealous of her husband because he had a life with her, something he'd likely never experience with Riley. While he couldn't expect her to give away her heart again, he could have this moment with her. After what he'd experienced in the last year, he'd learned no one held the promise of tomorrow.

After pleasuring her, he pulled her close, loving the feel of her breath against his bare skin. Loved that she'd asked for what she wanted. Loved that she'd been bold enough for them both.

From here on, he'd be the one to drive their

lovemaking. That way she'd have no doubt how much he wanted her. He glanced at the clock, Midnight, and she had to get up for work in a few hours. The thought of leaving flashed through his brain for only a second. There was no way in hell that was happening. He was ready to wake up next to the woman he wanted to spend the next hundred years with.

Even now his body begged for more. Much as it killed him, he shifted to the far side of the bed. It was the only way he could stay this close to her naked body.

Chapter Nine

Riley woke cold and naked. As she reached for the body she prayed was still there, the scream of little used muscles reminded her of what they'd done last night. Not that she could forget making love with Brian for one second. While the lust he inspired wasn't a new emotion, the courage she found to express it was. She wasn't sure she'd even been herself last night, her actions were so wanton. As were the delicious way he'd responded.

When her hand found only cold sheets, her pleasant memories of the night before crashed around her. Riley opened her eyes to find Brian was indeed still in the bed, but not by much. Facing away from her, he huddled against the far wall.

Anger roiled inside her, not just at him for not leaving if he regretted what they'd done, but at her own stupidity for thinking Brian wanted her. Riley bolted from her bed, grabbing a skirt and blouse from her closet on the way to the shower. At least she could salvage a little of her pride by being gone when he woke.

Minutes later she wiggled into clothes, her body still damp from the world's fastest shower. Before she slipped from her bedroom, her gaze darted to her bed. The sheet had slipped to Brian's hips, exposing his heavily muscled back. Her steps slowed, despite her desire to flee. The fact the two of them should have never gotten together was as evident as the scars etched on his golden skin.

The coffee pot called to her as she passed through the kitchen. She ignored it, instead reaching for her purse and keys. All she had to do was reach the garage and she'd be home free.

"Why didn't you wake me?"

Her shoulders slumped. "I thought I'd save us both the embarrassment of the dreaded walk of shame."

"Come again?" His sultry voice came from close behind, sending a shiver of desire dancing up her spine.

She couldn't find the courage to turn around. "Why didn't you just do us both a favor and leave?"

His arms fenced her in, preventing her escape.

God, she just couldn't catch a break with him.

"I saw the way you were huddled on the bed like you couldn't get far enough away from me." Angry tears stung the back of her eyes. "I don't have to be experienced to know pity sex when I get it." She silently cursed herself, even now as angry as she was, her body responded to him as he pinned her against the counter.

"Let's make one thing clear." He grounded his hips into her backside. "Does that feel like pity to you?"

When she didn't answer, he reached around to cup her breasts. "Answer me." His hands traveled across her body. "Does anything about what I'm doing to you feel like pity?'

"No."

He fisted her skirt, pushing it up her thighs. Then his palms slid down her hips. "I'm going to make damn sure you have no doubt how I feel about you."

Melissa Klein

The lovemaking was nothing like she'd experienced. Urgent. Needful. Consuming. When they'd both come back into their bodies, he pulled away. The fact they were both clothed, except for the places where their bodies met added to the elicit feeling of their tryst. The how and where of their joining was of no concern to her. In this moment she was wanted. She turned to press her cheek against his chest. When she'd committed his warm, masculine scent to memory, she tilted her chin to look at him. "You've made me late for work."

The corner of his mouth crooked up. "Is that a complaint?"

A blush heated her cheeks. "No, but now I have to face your sister and best friend. I don't think I can keep this silly look off my face."

Brian brushed his thumb across her cheek. "I don't think either one of them will care that we're together. In fact, Grant was the one who goaded me into making a bid on your donation."

"Remind me to thank him." Riley quickly came to the next round of hurdles she faced. "Maggie knows where you were last night."

"Yes, and she'll be glad for us."

She shook her head. "Your sister's very protective of her family."

He hugged her tighter. "If anything, she'll be worried about you. I don't exactly have a good track record with women."

His words gave her a moment of worry. In the next breath he laid them to rest. "This feels different though. You feel different."

Her heart swelled with emotion. She stood on

110

tiptoe, kissing him on the corner of his mouth. "It does for me as well." Riley still loved her husband but entwined in Brian's strong arms she was open to the possibility of loving another man, too.

****

"Sorry I'm late." Though she wasn't at all sorry her morning had taken a turn for the better after the God-awful way it started. When she didn't get a response from Maggie, Riley zeroed in on her friend's expression, looking for some indication to her mood. Hopefully, by giving into her attraction to Brian, she hadn't gained a lover but lost a friend.

Maggie's lips pressed together in a hard line and her brow furrowed, an expression she reserved for FAA inspectors, salesmen, and Grant's ex-wife.

An explanation hovered on Riley's lips, but anything she could say to explain her still evolving relationship with Brian seemed trite, juvenile, or too much information. "I'll have those reports ready for you today. I only have receivables left to do."

"I need them in the next hour." Maggie's matter of fact tone matched her pinched expression. "Remember I'm flying the rest of the week."

Riley nodded. "I'll have them finished by then."

Bypassing the coffee pot, Riley dove into the reports and had them ready well before the promised time. Afterward, she buried herself in other tasks, determined to keep her mind on her job. Though she and Brian smoothed a few of the wrinkles caused by the sudden change in their relationship it didn't mean all their problems were behind them. Her thoughts shot to the less than friendly greeting she'd gotten from Maggie. What if she took exception to her friend sleeping with her brother?

Riley shook her head. Deciding she'd cross that bridge when she got to it, she redoubled her efforts to concentrate on her work.

"Do you have a minute?"

Riley glanced at the monitor's clock, surprised to find her strategy worked and it was nearly noon. She swiveled in her chair to answer Grant's question. "What's up?"

Lord, please let this conversation be less awkward than the one I had with Maggie.

He leaned against the wall of her cubicle. "First, great job on the Victory for Veterans weekend. You and Brainstorm did a hellava good job."

At the mention of her lover's name, her pulse kicked up a notch. "It was a lot of fun. I really enjoyed working with Brian." Not as much as she enjoyed making love to him. She could still feel the way his arms had caged her as he took her against her kitchen counter. Riley shook her head to get her mind where it needed to be. "Working with Heather was great, too."

Grant arched an eyebrow. "She speaks very highly of you as well." He took a step further inside her cubicle. "That brings me to my main question. Are you happy here at Davis Air?"

"Absolutely." She'd half expected him to ask that very question. On more than one occasion during Riley's visits to Mountain View, she'd hinted she had an opening she'd like Riley to fill.

"Heather called this morning to warn me she was going to poach you from me. How much should I be worried?"

She shook her head. "None at all." Under different

circumstances she might have been tempted away. Before reconnecting with Jake, she'd job-hopped all over the Midwest pursuing any new and tantalizing offer. "I like Heather and her set up is great, but I have no plans to leave." Especially after this morning.

"So, you're not going to take off for the hills?"

Brian leaned through the opening of her cubicle. "I'd like to hear the answer to that myself."

"Hey, my man. What brings you here?" Grant pounded his back.

He crossed his arms, stretching his snug T-shirt across his biceps. "I was going to see if someone could shake off the chains of gainful employment long enough to have lunch with me."

"Really?" Grant's attention bounced between her and Brian.

"First, I want Riley to answer the question." His gaze locked on hers. "Are you going to bolt for the hills?"

Her response took no thought. "No. I'm very happy here."

Brian's arms fell to his side and the tension in his jaw eased.

His need for reassurance surprised her nearly as much as his unexpected appearance. He projected such self-confidence she'd have never guessed his uncertainty. One more way they were alike. His continued stare didn't surprise her, though. He communicated so much with his eyes while saying so little. Riley gripped the arm of her chair to keep from walking into his embrace as his gaze suggested. Thankfully, with the assurance Riley wasn't going to quit, Grant left them alone.

On their way out the door, Brian stopped at his sister's desk. "Riley and I are going to Mackenzie's Diner for lunch. Can we bring you back something, Magpie?"

Maggie shot him a narrow-eyed look. "No, I brought my lunch."

On the way out the door, Brian stage whispered. "She hates when I call her that."

Riley swatted his arm. "I don't think you should provoke her. I don't want to get on her bad side and neither should you." She decided to hash things out with Maggie when she got back from lunch. If her relationship with Brian was going to be a problem, she needed to find out now.

I don't know what I'll do if it is, but at least I'll know where I stand.

Out in the parking lot, Brian took her in his arms. "God, I missed you." He kissed her like they'd been apart for months.

Breathless both from the intensity of his kiss and the sheer joy of being with him, she gasped. "You just saw me a couple hours ago."

"Can't you see I'm insatiable, sunshine?"

The nickname didn't suit her, even with the lighter than air feeling she was experiencing. "Why do you call me that? I'm hardly Polly Anna."

"Your skin looks sun kissed for one thing." His eyes were hooded as he pressed a kiss to her shoulder. "You also have a way of chasing away that little black cloud that's been over my head since the accident."

He'd done the same for her, making her happier than she deserved. "I'm glad."

After grabbing a sandwich at the diner, they were

back at the airport before she was ready. She lingered in his car.

He must have felt the same since when she reached for the door handle, he stilled her hand. "Come hang out with the kids and me after work tonight."

"I can't." She wanted nothing more than to shirk her commitments in favor of time with him. In the space of hours, he'd barged in and realigned her priorities.

His thumb traced over the back of her hand. "Come on. I know you like the two little hellions."

"I do, but Abby and another client are coming over to work out."

"I like the way you and I work out." He pulled her in to him.

"I do too, but your sister might not want us hanging out if you're going do that."

Brian arched an eyebrow. "What if I promise to be on my best behavior?"

He was a temptation she couldn't resist. "It would be late before I could get there."

The corner of his mouth turned up, probably relishing the fact he'd won her over again. "Are you kidding? Lexi and Matt are in full summer mode. I'll be lucky to get them in bed before midnight."

"I'll call after Mrs. Patterson leaves."

Back inside the office, Riley made a beeline for Maggie. She set a milkshake on her desk. "I brought you back something." She hoped it would ease the transition into what could be a tricky conversation.

"Do you have that report I asked for?"

She pointed to the computer. "Should be in your inbox." When Maggie turned to face the screen, Riley figured it was better to get things out in the open than to have this weirdness between them. "Do you have a problem with Brian and me seeing each other?"

"If I did, would you stop?" Maggie fixed her with a stare.

Nothing like cutting to the heart of the matter.

"I don't know." The last thing she wanted was to lose a friend, but she couldn't walk away from Brian. He got her in ways others didn't. "I like him a lot so probably not." She met her friend's gaze. "I'd ask you to keep an open mind though."

"That was so bitchy of me." The corners of her mouth turned up. "I wanted to see if you were really into my brother."

Riley let out a breath. Uncertainty tempered her relief. They both carried a lot of baggage that had the potential to bury them. "I don't know where this is going, but I'm not the type to dive into a relationship if I don't think it's got potential."

Maggie nodded. "That's what I thought, but Brian's never had a serious girlfriend so don't get scared if he backs away."

That had been Riley's worry as she'd left him standing in her kitchen that morning but showing up at the hangar had gone a long way towards easing that fear. "He asked me to come over to your place and hang out with the kids. If you're not comfortable with that, I understand."

"Matt and Lexi think you hung the moon. Why would that bother me?"

"I wasn't certain how you felt about them knowing about their uncle and me. I'm not going to spend the night or anything."

"That wouldn't be a problem if you did. Believe it or not, I've dated since their father and I divorced. I'm sorry you thought I wasn't cool with you and Brian. The fact is, I'm wigging out about the kids seeing their dad."

"Brian mentioned them leaving in the morning."

"Yeah, they're going to spend a couple weeks with him. They haven't seen Rob in nearly three years. Matt has some memory of us being a family, but Lexi doesn't. She's seven for crying out loud, I'm not sure she even remembers what the man looks like. Now she has to spend two weeks with the guy."

Her heart clenched. "Are you worried about their safety?"

Maggie shook her head. "Rob isn't like that. He is unreliable and couldn't stick to a schedule if his life depended on it. I'm worried what it will do to them when he drops off the radar again."

"I can't say I understand what it's like to leave your kids with someone you don't completely trust." Riley clasped Maggie's hand. "But I do know what it's like to have to live with a stranger."

Maggie shot Riley a hopeful look. "Will you talk to them if they bring it up? I've tried but I don't' know what to say."

"Sure."

"You're a godsend, you really are." Maggie grasped her in a hard hug.

She was certain she hadn't been divinely sent to Magnolia Springs, but in that moment she was willing to do pretty much anything to keep herself in the first place that felt like home in years.

Chapter Ten

Riley barely had Gloria parked when Matt and Lexi poured out of the house. They crawled over the sides of the car and into the backseat. "Uncle Brian says we're going for ice cream."

"I know isn't that exciting." In truth, what got her pulse going was the man stalking towards her. His heavy arms swung at his side like he had a mission to complete. He leaned over the door and kissed her. With the part of her brain not occupied with relishing the feel of his firm lips against hers, she marveled how much had changed since she woke.

"Eeeewww." Matt groaned from the backseat. "That's gross."

Brian scrubbed his nephew's head. "Give it three or four years and you won't think so, wild man." With that, Brian crossed the front of the car, taking the passenger seat.

A tap on Riley's shoulder pulled her attention from considering the sinful things Brian did to a T-shirt. "What's up, Lexi?"

The seven-year-old had a way of studying a person that called to mind how the girl's mother had eyeballed Riley that morning. "Do you like my Uncle Brian?"

"I do."

"What's not to like," Brian chimed in.

"No." Lexi folded her arms across her tiny chest.

"Do you like him, like him?"

Riley bit her lip to keep from laughing. She leaned over the seat so the little girl could see her seriousness. "I totally like him, like him."

Lexi nodded as if that settled the matter.

"Put on your seatbelts, kiddos. We're heading for the open road."

Following Brian's directions, Riley steered Gloria onto the highway leading out of Magnolia Springs. "This used to be the main road between Atlanta and Columbia, South Carolina. Can you imagine? I bet it took forever to get there." Brian continued with the history lesson.

Riley would take the hours and want more. Flying down the road with two kids in the back seat and a handsome man by her side, she was living someone else's life. She couldn't shake the feeling she'd wake up any minute and realize it was simply another one of her dreams. Unlike the ones that had her waking in a cold sweat, this was one from which she never wanted to wake. It was too perfect to be real and too perfect to last. Brian grasped her nape with his strong hands massaging her neck.

A round of *Ninety-nine Bottles of Pop on the Wall* later, they pulled into a root beer stand and a girl skated up. While waiting for their ice cream Riley tackled the promise she'd made to Maggie. She turned to Matt and Lexi. "I hear you two are going on vacation with your dad in the morning."

"Yeah." Matt's eyes sparked. His sister didn't look as if she shared her brother's excitement.

Riley tapped into the myriad of worries she'd had as a child. Once she was placed in the children's home and met Jake things got better. "Remember you've got each other and I'm sure your dad will let you call your mom anytime you like."

That seemed to ease Lexi's worries because when the ice creamed arrived, she dove in with reckless enthusiasm.

After the ice cream and a dozen choruses of *On Top of Old Smokey,* the four of them pulled into Maggie's driveway. "Good night," she called to Matt and Lexi as they ran towards the house. "Have fun in Florida."

"You're leaving?"

"It's late and the kids have a big day ahead of them."

He threaded his fingers with hers. "Stay a while longer."

"I don't want you to get tired of me."

He snaked an arm around her, pulling her in tight. "Tired of you? I can't get enough."

Riley tried to use what was left of her common sense. "I'm sure you've got things you need to do before tomorrow. Besides, I feel like I'm intruding."

"You've said that several times. Get this through that beautiful-but-hard head of yours, you're wanted. By Grant and Abby, Maggie and the kids…" He caught her gaze. "Me."

She had no resistance when it came to this man. A smile played at the corner of her mouth. "I'm beginning to see that. Okay, I'll stay."

They followed Matt and Lexi through the house and onto their screened in porch. As the kids took off for the back yard, Brian led Riley to a swing. "Do they catch fireflies every night?" She watched Matt and Lexi race around the yard.

"It's a nightly ritual, and here in the south we call them lightening bugs." He stretched the word to multiple syllables.

"What do you southerners do with these critters?" She mimicked his sultry drawl.

"Let them go." He wrapped his arm around her shoulder.

The two of them rocked in the swing for several minutes without speaking. Lexi fluttered around the yard chasing after the little sparks, while Matt stalked the insects. When he succeeded in catching one, he made a beeline to show his sister before letting it loose. That respect for creatures and little sisters had to be taught. Riley's heart warmed even as it grieved. She'd seen too many incidents of humanity's capacity for cruelty during her time in foster care.

"How do you like playing house?" Brian nuzzled into her hair.

He'd sensed it too, this act they were performing. Unwilling to let go of the fiction, she sidestepped his questions. "They are great kids. You should be proud."

Brian nodded. "Maggie's an awesome mom. I just try not to mess them up." He continued with the gentle circles he was massaging into her neck. "About last night."

Her stomach knotted. Given her history, she couldn't help the knee-jerk reaction any more than she could help wanting her time with him to last a little longer.

"Don't." He pried her palm loose from the swing and laced his fingers with hers. "It was wonderful." His soft croon made her insides go all warm and soft. "But we need to talk about a couple things before we do that again."

Riley turned to him, meaning to set him straight. "I'm not spending the night. Maggie and I already talked about that."

One corner of his mouth turned up. "My sister, the cockblocker." His face grew serious. "Things got pretty heated and I know I told you I was clean, but we should use protection next time."

Riley was very practical when it came to her body but having to explain why birth control was a non-issue wasn't high on her to-do list. "I can't get pregnant. Jake and I tried the whole time we were together. With both of us growing up without a family we knew we both wanted kids. It just never happened."

"Okay." Brian said with a matter of fact jerk of his chin. "That takes care of one question."

"I need to know if that's going to be a problem for you." Before he claimed any more of her heart, she had to know how her infertility impacted their chances for a long-term relationship. Her gaze shot to Lexi and Matt. "I can tell you love kids. Did you ever want your own?"

Seconds ticked by before he answered. "I never gave it much thought." He released her hand to rub his palms against his denim clad thighs. "I've never been in a relationship so pregnancy has always been something to avoid. I guess I'm okay with being the favorite uncle."

The tightness in Riley's chest eased. Though they wanted different things at least those differences weren't going to get in the way. "What was the other question you wanted to ask?"

"I forgot." He shook his head. "I tend to do that a

lot when I'm around you."

"Is that a good thing?"

His gaze darted to the back yard where the kids were still catching lightening bugs. Then he pressed his lips to hers in a kiss that started off sweet and ended with heat. When he finally released her, they were both breathless. "Believe me it's a very good thing."

With several potential problems averted all the tension left her body. It didn't guarantee she wouldn't still get her heart broken, but at least she had a better idea where she stood. She leaned into his shoulder. "Lovely kids, lovely man." Perhaps it was the combination of the swing and his warm body that loosened her lips. "Everything here seems so perfect."

"We're a far from perfect family. Just wait until you see me try to get those two inside for the night then you'll see just how imperfect we are."

Riley raised her head to look up at him. Though he'd made the statement in a joking way, the tension in his jaw gave him away. "I know that. But there's so much love here."

The hand that had been gently caressing her hair stilled. "Won't you tell me something about yourself? It feels strange to know how beautiful your bare body is and know so little about you. At least tell me more about your childhood."

Riley shook her head. "I remember little of the time before I was left at the children's home and what I do recall isn't worth talking about. I don't want it to taint our perfect evening."

"Our father used to beat Maggie and I with a riding crop."

Brian's statement hung in the air and she had to

swallow hard against the bile rising in her throat. For all that Riley's childhood had lacked, at least she'd never been abused. That didn't mean she hadn't seen the effects of it from the other children living at the home. She squeezed his hand in silent encouragement. As little as she wanted to hear how two people she cared about were mistreated, she got a sense he needed to share this part of himself with her.

"It didn't matter if our infraction was a forgotten chore or a perceived show of disrespect, the punishment was the same. Only the number of licks changed according to some demerit chart in General Stone's head. See, he carried his methods of disciplining his men over into his home." Brian stilled the swing. "The man never hit us in anger. The punishments were carried out in an orderly and dispassionate manner. He said the world was a harsh place and if we wanted to amount to anything Maggie and I needed to learn discipline."

Emotion choked her and it was several seconds before she could speak. "God, that's so horrible."

"With Maggie and I having such a crappy example of raising children, I've never wanted kids of my own." He cupped her face. "I didn't tell you that because I wanted your sympathy or to pressure you to reciprocate. I wanted you to know the reality behind all this perfect you see."

"I know that. But even if Matt and Lexi started WW III and you lost your cool and threatened to ground them till they were forty, you'd still be a perfect family because you love each other."

The kids picked that moment to act on Riley's prediction. A wail erupted from the shadows, followed by the scramble of two pairs of feet. "I should get going."

"Wait. This won't take but a second." He thumbed over his shoulder. "You two, inside." When the kids were out of sight he pulled her in close. "Will you stay? They're spending the night at friends."

"I have an idea." She spoke as her plan took shape. "But only if you want to, if not, it's no big deal."

Brian squeezed her tight. "Haven't you figured out by now I'm up for anything?"

His boldness was rubbing off on her. "After you get Matt and Lexi situated with their dad, come stay a few days with me at my place."

"And what would we do during these few days?" He waggled his eyebrows.

Despite being a nearly forty-one years old and their having made love twice already, her cheeks heated at his suggestion. "I thought we could work out. Maybe do a couple sessions a day. Really get you up to speed."

"I'll see you as soon as I get the kids squared away."

****

After pulling her phone from her purse, Riley shot a text to Brian letting him know she'd made it home.

What a worrywart.

Before she could set her phone on the kitchen counter, he responded with a reminder to lock the doors. She smiled, despite how unnecessary his concern was. Knowing someone cared was a nice, if unaccustomed, feeling. One she could too easily learn to love.

Despite the late hour, restlessness kept Riley cleaning her already tidy kitchen. She unloaded the dishwasher and mopped before she'd unwound enough to feel the number of hours she'd been up.

Passing through the dining room, she eyed the paint can and brushes. When she'd started working on the project yesterday she'd been certain she'd never see Brian again. Now she had to figure out how not to screw things up. With their collective past between them, it was optimistic to think they had much chance of sticking out a relationship for the long haul. That was before she factored in the likelihood the job Brian was applying for would relocate him. She'd just have to make the most of the time they did have.

Hearing a car pull into the driveway, Riley realized she was about to get a bonus on their time together. She made it to the front door as he raised his hand to knock.

"You don't look surprised to see me." His full lips curved in a sensual smile.

"I'm not." She noted his duffle bag as it hit the foyer floor. "Patience isn't one of your strong suits."

Brian pushed the door closed, and then backed her into the nearest wall with his kisses. "With the promise of this, how could I be expected to wait?"

Even if his erection hadn't been pressing into the soft part of her belly, Riley would have known what he'd hoped to achieve by showing up. The way he continued to nibble her neck spoke of a hunger not easily sated.

He wasn't the only one whose appetite had been awakened. The thoughts of making love with him had Riley tugging his T-shirt from his jeans. She stopped though, changing tactics. The two times they'd been together were need-driven expressions of their lust for each other. She wanted to seduce him.

Riley stepped out of his embrace, placing a palm against his chest when he went to tug her back. "I want to freshen up a bit first. I'll meet you in the bedroom in a few minutes.

Riley got a step towards acting on her intent before Brian snagged her hand. He drew her in, snaking his hands around her waist. "Bossy much?" He brushed aside her hair to nip her ear.

"Every chance I get." Riley closed the bathroom door. The glaring lights over the sink revealed his effect on her. Her cheeks were bright, visible even with her warm complexion and her pupils had dilated to the point only a small ring of violet showed. She took several steadying breaths, wishing she was better at hiding her feelings when it came to him.

Having something short and sexy to wear to bed wouldn't be a bad thing either. After stripping out of her clothes, she took the over-sized T-shirt she wore to bed off its hook. She'd gotten it a couple years ago for participating in a road race in some small town she was living in at the time. After brushing her teeth and scrubbing her face, she'd done as much as she could towards making herself more appealing to him.

Riley opened the door leading to her bedroom to find Brian had followed her instructions. Propped against the headboard, he lay in the middle of her bed. His bare chest got her moving quickly across the floor. She loved the contrast of his supple skin against the hard plane of his chest.

After slipping under the covers, she switched off the bedside lamp and snuggled into his body.

"Wait a minute." He leaned over her to turn the light back on. "I want to appreciate what I've waited all this time for."

Unease had her fisting the sheet. Her plans to seduce him wouldn't work if he was worried about his legs. "I wasn't sure how you liked it."

He studied her for a moment, making her wonder what was going on behind those gorgeous hazel eyes of his. His face gave so little away while hers kept nothing back.

"I've made a point of hiding my injuries from people." His thumb traced over her cheek, causing her heart to clench at his tenderness. "You get me. You get that I'm more than what was done to me."

Tears welled in her eyes and she had to look away or she'd lose it all together. "How am I supposed to seduce you if my nose is all red from crying?"

Brian grasped her shoulders, turning her to face him. "All it takes to make me your love slave is one crook of your finger."

After they made love, he held her close, as if he sensed she needed his body to ground her. He got her as well. Understood what she needed more than anyone in a longtime. In understanding what made her tick, Brian Stone stripped her bare to the soul. The flip side was he also had the power to hurt her. The realization had her turning away. Pulling the covers to her shoulder, she scooted to the edge of the bed.

"Not a chance." He tugged her back. "I'm not going anywhere and neither are you." He settled her so that her cheek rested over his heart. Soon the steady rhythm settled her and she was finally able to drift off to sleep.

Chapter Eleven

"Please, don't leave me."

The guttural plea snatched Brian from his sleep. "Shh." He tried to still Riley's thrashing body.

"I'm sorry." Tears spilled down her cheeks.

"Wake up." His gut told him what she could not. Taking a lover had kicked up memories of her husband. And elicit emotions she didn't need to feel. Guilt was a powerful tormentor, one that had him in its grips all too often. He switched on the bedside lamp. When she didn't respond, he took her by the shoulders. "Open your eyes."

She complied, blinking several times. "Oh, God." She lowered her head.

Brian wrapped his arms around her. "You were having a nightmare."

His heart ached for her, wishing he could do something to erase her pain. He'd experienced the same loss of power, of being utterly cast adrift in memories. His own private hell arrived while he was fully awake, like at the park. Flashbacks overtook him with little warning, something he wouldn't wish on his worst enemy much less this beautiful woman who clung to him. He tilted her chin. "Everything's fine."

She gripped his shoulders, her nails biting into his flesh.

"That's it. You're here with me, now."

Her hand slid below the sheets to his hips. His breath escaped in a hiss. He'd gladly make love to her for hours, days, if that was what she needed. He pressed his lips to hers as if to draw the darkness from her.

Riley broke the kiss. "Please make love to me."

Brian obeyed her plea, pouring everything he had to give into her. When he'd drawn a release from her, he drew her in tight so their bodies melded. He nuzzled her cheek with his own, drawing in her scent as he breathed and worked to lessen the burning in his chest. This woman would be his undoing if he wasn't careful. Her body shook with what he thought were aftershocks until he felt something wet hit his cheek. Oh shit!" He pulled back so he could examine her. "Did I hurt you?"

She shook her head. "You took it all away."

Relief washed over him. "I'll never understand women. You say that like it's a bad thing."

Riley thumbed away her tears. "It's been a long time since I've felt this way and it's a little much to take in."

He knew where she was coming from. For days after he met her, the weightless sensation felt strange. He told her something he was still working through himself. "You have no reason to feel guilty either. If Jake was half the man I think he was, he'd want you to be happy. Just like my army buddies would want the same for me."

The corners of her mouth turned up. "I'm not sure I'm ready to be involved with a mind reader."

Involved. Hardly the word he'd use to describe the way he felt about Riley. A person got involved with clubs and charities. With her passion, her wit, and even her darkness, she consumed him.

Brian was only vaguely aware his fingers found their way to her hair. He hoped combing through the tresses soothed her the way it did him. "Tell me about your dream. Sometimes that helps."

She snuggled close so that her body molded to his. "Just hold me."

"As long as you'll let me."

Brian kept his promise, watching over Riley until sunlight chased away the night. They'd conquered more obstacles in the past few days than most couples did in a lifetime, and yet as he watched her sleep, they still had more hurdles and land minds ahead. If only he could keep her from leaving, he could love her guilt and doubts away.

Chapter Twelve

Riley slipped back into her bedroom at dawn. Light filtered through the blinds, turning the walls a warm pink, and illuminating the male body taking up most of the real estate of her queen-sized mattress. A week after inviting Brian to stay with her, the sight of him in her bed still seemed surreal.

It also stirred feelings in her she wasn't ready to identify. He mattered. More than she was comfortable admitting. She could easily get addicted to his thick arms wrapping around her or the feel of his warm breath tickling her neck as they dozed. Not that she spent a lot of time sleeping next to him. Twice daily workouts and mind-blowing sex hadn't cured her insomnia.

Bone-tired, she longed to join him, to nuzzle into his body for some much-needed rest. They'd fallen asleep entwined in each other. Then in the early morning hours the nightmares started. After waking drenched in sweat, she grabbed a pillow and a paperback and waited for the sun to rise.

After the first night Brian stayed, Riley was determined not to have a repeat performance. In her desperation to rid herself of the dream's aftereffects, she'd let slip the guilt that plagued her sleep. Brian didn't need her burden to add to his own.

Riley eased down to the mattress and watched

Brian sleep. She took in the hard edge of his jaw and his well-toned biceps as he hugged her pillow. Her fingers itched to touch his whisker-shadowed cheeks. With him resting she could almost see what he must have looked like before his life in the army took its toll. She couldn't imagine what would make a person want a job that required so much of himself. Jake called it a sense of duty, a need to see the weak were protected. If asked, Brian would most likely offer a similar answer.

Despite his assurances the job he worked towards was safe, a sense of dread haunted her. Where her daytime worries left off, her creative subconscious took over. Last night, instead of reliving Jake's death, her masochistic imagination coughed up a sequence of events leading up to her playing witness to Brian's death. Maybe not knowing where the new job would take him or where that would leave them was what triggered the new nightmare.

Riley shook her head, purposely changing the direction of her thoughts. This wasn't about her. She'd promised to help him reach his goal. After he passed the PT test there'd be time for them to evaluate where things were headed. If it was headed anywhere.

She touched his shoulder. "Rise and shine."

Brian answered with a groaned, "no." He slid his arms around her waist and buried his head in her lap. "Come back to bed."

It was tempting.

He was tempting. Uncertainty defined their future, but not the present. Memories of their lovemaking the night before flooded her brain making her ached to feel again the weight of him as he pressed her into the mattress. In those moments when their bodies came together, her past and his future ceased to exist.

Her hand inched its way along the bed, ready to act on her thoughts. If she tunneled beneath the sheets, she'd find him bare and in a few strokes she could give him the best wakeup call ever.

Riley clenched the covers. Brian was thirty seconds off the time necessary to pass his physical. "No, you need to get up. It'll be too hot to run by the time I get back home tonight."

He grinned up at her, his hazel eyes flashing with mischief. "I have an idea. Let's get our cardio here."

"Your PT test is in a few weeks." She was losing the battle to be the sensible one. The covers slid down to his hips as sat upright. The sight of his well-muscled chest only made her resolve that much tougher to hold.

Cupping her cheek, his face lost some of its animation. "My times have been good. Thanks to you. I really don't think we have anything to worry about."

They had three weeks until his interview and PT test. Twenty-one days in which she could kick his butt out of bed for a morning run. Riley held up a finger. "Just this once."

"I knew you'd see things my way." He kissed her down to the bed.

A naughty idea flashed in her brain. "Wait." She gripped his shoulders.

Brian grinned up at her, heat flashing in his eyes. "Don't tell me you don't want this, sunshine, because I distinctly remember you begging for it last night."

Brian Stone had one talented mouth. The temptation to let him take over their lovemaking was a relentless pull. "That's true." She ran her fingers over his brush cut. "But you've forgotten one thing. You sweet-talked your way into letting this count as your workout, so that makes me in charge."

"I love when you're bossy."

She did, too, even when it made her late for work again.

****

Riley tied off the wrapping paper filled trash bag, setting it outside the conference room door. With that she was finished cleaning up from the lunch-time bridal shower they'd thrown one of the other Davis Air Transport employees. Hardly a week went by that Maggie didn't think up some reason to celebrate. Today's was an especially fun excuse to hang out in the conference room. "I thought Truck was going to blow a gasket when Lindsey held up that lace teddy you got her," she told Maggie.

For the first few weeks of her employment at Davis Air Transport, Riley continued as she always had. She'd done the job she was paid to do, dropping off her personal life at the door on her way in and doing the same with her work world when she left at the end of the day.

Her friend slid the leftover cake inside the pink bakery box. "That was part of the fun."

The relentless force of inclusion that made up the atmosphere here made that tactic impossible to continue. For the first time, Riley felt connected to a group of people. Some days she couldn't wait to get to work so she could hear about Lindsey's wedding plans or what Matt and Lexi had done.

Maggie thrust the large pink box in Riley's direction. "Take this home to Brian. If I take it I'll eat the whole thing."

Her pulse kicked up a notch. She loved the sweet way Brian sent her off to work that morning with coffee and a kiss, but she wouldn't let herself take for granted she'd find him there when she got home. She held up her hands. "No way." Besides even if he was waiting for her, neither of them needed anymore decadence than what they enjoyed in each other's arms.

"I say we just toss it." She ran her finger inside the waist band of her trousers. Despite her twice daily workouts, her clothes were fitting a little snug lately. She'd be forty-one in the fall, maybe the couple extra pounds she'd put on were a sign of a slowing metabolism. Riley thought about the bride and how young she seemed.

"Is it just me, or does Lindsey seem too young to get married?" Maggie asked, reading Riley's mind.

"What is she, like twenty-two?"

"I think so." Maggie nodded. "She graduated from college back in June."

Riley remembered all too well when she'd been Lindsey's age. "Marriage was the last thing on my mind back then. I was in Chicago, trying to find myself. Man, I wish I could have a word with twenty-two-year-old me." She could have saved herself a lot of time since the members of her birth family whom she'd found in Chicago hadn't been worth finding. Then the realization no one was out there looking for her had been another blow that had taken many years to heal.

"I hear you. The corners of her mouth turned up. "I was fresh out of the Air Force Academy and thought I was all that and a bag of chips." She paused her recollection, looking at Riley with a gleam in her eye. "Did you talk my brother into coming with you to the wedding?"

"I did." She was still trying to wrap her brain around the fact people assumed she and Brian were a couple. Long ago, she learned not to assume anything. Not that she had a family who wanted her, or that the people she cared about would be there when she returned at the end of the day. Most importantly, she'd learned just because she had feelings for someone, that didn't necessarily mean they returned those emotions. Not knowing where she stood with Brian hadn't kept her from enjoying what she had right now. Coercing him into attending had been fun, despite how much he protested. "He said he wasn't anxious to see one of his high school buddies playing father of the bride. But I got him to see things my way in the end." Her method of changing his mind led to them missing their evening workout.

Maggie arched an eyebrow. "Maybe you'll catch the bouquet."

"I don't know if I'm ready for that." Riley's eyes widened. She might never be ready to get married again. Not that he was asking.

The number eleven took shape between Maggie's eyebrows. "Are things not going well with Brian?" She touched Riley's shoulder. "Please be patient. I've been trying to domesticate him since he moved in with me, but he's a work in progress."

"No, he's great. I just want to take things slow. I've been on my own so much it's hard to imagine living any other way."

"Well, cake or no cake, I say it's time for you to go home to him."

Riley nodded. "You're probably right. I left him on

the treadmill this morning. I wonder what he's gotten up to since then."

"I think you may be surprised."

Minutes later, Riley eased Gloria into traffic. See even inanimate objects could let a person down. Her everyday car wouldn't start that morning.

Aren't I Debbie Downer today?

Would she be more optimistic if her childhood had been different? Despite telling people she didn't remember her early years, Riley had a much clearer memory than she wished. Most times she didn't allow herself to dwell on the days before she was taken to Bethany Children's Home where she met Jake. The image of Auntie Bess popped into her head. *Wow!* She hadn't thought about her in years. When Riley's birth mother walked away from her, social services really had to dig to find a relative willing to take on the care of a toddler. When the paternal elderly great-aunt grew too old to care for Riley, social services stepped in again, placing her in a series of foster homes.

By the time she pulled Gloria into her driveway, Riley had worked herself into a total funk. The sight of Brian's car helped a little. She entered her back door and a myriad of scents overtook her. Something beefy was cooking in the oven and chemical fumes wafted in from the other side of the house. But the best smell of all filled her sense as Brian walked in from the enclosed garage where her gym was. "Lucy, I'm home," she said in her best fake Cuban accent.

"It's about damned time, woman." He scooped her up in an all-encompassing hug.

She nuzzled into his neck. Even as she relished the moment, she couldn't let herself grow complacent, to expect he'd be there when she came home at the end of the day. In all the conversations they'd had, not once had they discussed anything beyond his job interview and PT test. When his reasons for needing her were gone would he as well? She pulled back. God, she could look into his fierce hazel eyes and never once fail to appreciate them.

The swirl of brown and green mixed with flecks of gold touched her soul because she saw beyond the color to the pain behind the warrior's stare. When they'd first met, she couldn't imagine even being friends with the guy. His darkness seemed too close to her own for them to be any kind of a match. Now, she couldn't imagine not having him in her life. That scared the holy crap out of her, made pins and needles go all over her scalp. "I see you've been busy." She hoped her light and breezy fooled him. He didn't deserve to have to put up with her melancholy mood.

Brian shrugged then tugged her into the dining room. The walls she began painting a week ago and abandoned when he'd shown up at her door were painted a happy shade of yellow. "I got tired of hanging around all day waiting for you to come home, so I thought I'd finish what you started. You don't like it?"

Riley shook her head. "It's great." Emotion tightened her throat.

He'd also hung curtains in the windows and set the table, making the whole room seem like more than simply a place to eat without propping the dinner plate on her lap.

Riley drew in a deep breath to ease the tightness in her chest. He was giving her more than a finished home improvement project or even the warmth of another body to cuddle next to in bed. He grounded her.

"What?" He took her in his arms. "Something's obviously bothering you."

If she didn't expect good things, happy things that other people took for granted, then she was never disappointed. But she wanted it all: community, friends, family. *Brian*. Riley looked into the face of the man who could give it all to her. And could take it away if he wanted. "I'm just surprised, that's all." She couldn't put herself in that position again. Of loving someone and having them hurt her. Even if they didn't mean to. Before every shift, Riley had sent Jake off with a kiss after extracting a promise that he'd be careful. Good intentions hadn't helped him keep his promise.

His brows knitted. "You'll let me know if I overstep my bounds."

Riley caressed his shoulders. "Of course." It wasn't his fault she found risking her heart again terrifying. She flashed him a smile as she stepped from his embrace. "Let's see if you can beat me in the mile."

"Loser cleans the kitchen."

****

Brian stepped into Riley's living room. She hadn't heard him enter since she was lost in one of her books. It made for the perfect opportunity to watch her since any other time he tried to take her in, she ducked her head or redirected his attention with kisses.

Her long, nearly black hair hung loose, covering her shoulders like a waterfall. Her honey-colored skin had warmed over the summer to a golden brown. "Here you go, babe." He glanced down at the bowl of ice cream as he handed it to her, thinking like dessert, one taste of her and he was hooked.

"You know this undoes about half of our workout." She took the bowl from him.

"Somehow, I doubt that. You pushed me hard tonight." Brian took his spot next to her, turning up the volume on the ball game playing on her tiny T.V. He drew her into his body, acting on the urging of his inner caveman.

Mine!

He let himself drink in the feeling of her body as she nestled into him. Now he knew why men did crazy things like climb water towers to paint their girl's name or go all DIY and paint her dining room. Having someone who got him, or didn't try to change him, made a guy think white picket fence thoughts.

"Mind if I change the channel? I wanted to catch the news." His contact at Mobletech sent an email asking him to watch a report hitting the networks.

"Go ahead. I'm more into this book than who is ahead in the NL east." Riley went back to her e-reader, and he switched the set to one of the cable outlets.

Thirty seconds in Brian knew why Mac had him watching. Reports were surfacing of Al-Qaeda infiltrating the tri-border area , a section of jungle where the borders of Argentina, Bolivia, and Paraguay met.

"It looks like America's enemies are joining forces," the reporter dressed in khaki safari garb stated. "Question is, how will this affect our safety at home."

"It won't make it safer that's for damn sure." Every time the U.S. thought they got one fire under control another hot spot flared. All he could do was watch from the sidelines.

Riley gripped his hand. "Can the army call you

back and send you there?" Anxiety shadowed her face.

"No, sunshine, that's nothing for you to worry about."

Brian switched the T.V. back to the sports channel. What he didn't say, was that if given half a chance he'd be on the next plane to the hot zone. The closest he'd come to seeing South America was the briefs he'd get if he got hired on a Mobletech. He suspected the military contractor might be acting as unofficial advisors to the pro-democratic forces in the area, doing what the U.S. couldn't.

Minutes later Brian was pulled from his musing. The screen of Riley's e-reader darkened, and he looked down to see she'd fallen asleep. He watched her at peace, a sight he couldn't get enough of. But not long after, her steady breaths became more rapid and her muscles twitched.

His gut twisted; his girl couldn't catch a break even taking a nap. Had the news report set her off? Or was it him? While Riley brought out the best in him, he couldn't say he did the same for her. Rather than dissipating into the ether, it seemed she absorbed his darkness.

"Riley, baby, wake up. You're dreaming."

She jerked. "What?"

"Why don't you go on to bed?" He tugged her to her feet then waited while she did her thing in the bathroom. Afterward, when he had her tucked under the covers, he pressed a kiss to her forehead.

She grabbed his hand when he moved from the bed. "Leave the dishes. I'll get them in the morning."

He laced his fingers through hers. "I was thinking I'd head back to my place tonight."

"Why?" Her grip on him tightened. "The kids aren't due back for another week."

"I don't think this is a good idea." At least not for her.

"What? Us?" Panic colored her voice, making him feel like a heel for adding to her troubles.

"No, me staying over. I mean, how good can it be if I'm causing these nightmares."

"It's not you. I've had them for years. I've told you that."

"But you've had one every night." She probably thought he didn't know she went to the living room after the dreams started. He'd played along, hoping not to make things worse by calling attention to them.

Tears welled in her eyes before she turned her head. "I'm sorry. I must be keeping you up." She tugged her hand from him, crossing her arms across her chest. "No wonder you're ready for your own bed."

He pulled her onto his lap. "It's not that. I'm worried I'm pushing you too hard and you're going to push back." Brian knew that defensive tactic. It was one he frequently employed.

"Don't go. I like having you here."

He buried his nose in her hair, breathing in the coconut scent of her shampoo and willing her to open to him. "Then tell me about your dreams."

She tensed in his embrace. "I can't"

Then he would. "It starts the same way it always does. Some mundane event you've done a thousand times. Then suddenly you're watching your life explode around you. You watch as people you care about bleed out, die. There isn't a goddamned thing you can do about it. No matter how hard you try you can't change what happened, not even in your dreams."

Brian tightened his grip as her shoulders began to shake. Whatever else he fucked up, she'd know he was there to ground her. He didn't say anymore, just kept up with the steady circles he was making on her back. She'd talk when she got ready.

After a moment, she looked up at him from those dark lashes of hers. "God, how did you get inside my head?"

He tilted her chin to meet his gaze. "I didn't. That's my nightmare and I clung to it, feeling it was my due for living when others didn't. You've changed that, brought sunshine into my nightmares. The past can't hurt us if we don't let it."

Her shoulders slumped. "I have this sick premonition something bad is about to happen."

"We're happy, you and me. You think something's going to come along and take that away. You and I are alike in a lot of ways. We've been hurt and not anxious to let that happen again. Let me assure you of one thing, I'm going to get out of bed each day and do my damnedest not to mess this up." While he was on a roll, he was going to get another thing out in the open. "And something else, dear one." He didn't often pull out the big guns with her. "The next time you have a nightmare, you will wake me." He used a finger to tilt her chin so he could look her in the eye. "You will let me comfort you. Is that clear?"

Pain flashed in her eyes. "But what happens when they come and you're not here?"

Brian thought of the interview coming up. Saying he'd be there at the end of the day like he'd none for the last week was a promise he couldn't make. Best case scenario, he'd be in the field for weeks at a time, with breaks where he'd come back to Magnolia Springs. "God, baby." He kissed her hard so she'd know just how serious he was. With his lips still on hers he promised, "You just have to trust that even if I'm not there at that moment in time, I'm going to do everything I can to get back to you."

She responded to his kiss, deepening it till their tongues were fighting for dominance. "Then start by getting in this bed with me, and let's not have any more talking about you going back to your place."

He could totally do that. They spent most of the night not talking, at least not with words anyway. Brian was better with actions than words anyway.

Chapter Thirteen

Riley checked her watch. Another few minutes and she could call this day a success. All that needed to happen was for Brian to return in one piece and she'd be the most relieved woman on the planet.

"Would you like more iced tea?"

Riley looked up at Abby. Following shopping and lunch at a cute bistro, the two women returned to Abby's house in Decatur to wait for their guys to return from their motorcycle ride.

"Excuse me." She hadn't meant to ignore her hostess and hoped her lack of attention hadn't been obvious. She enjoyed getting to know her boss' wife during their workouts, and their girls' day was a pleasant diversion considering what Brian and Grant were up to.

"Iced tea." Abby held up the pitcher.

She raised her glass. "Thanks." After her friend topped off her glass, she set it back on the patio table. *It will be fine. He knows what he's doing.*

"They'll be back soon."

Abby's knowing smile eased her nerves. "Am I that obvious?"

Maggie touched her hand. "Only because I know how you feel. Believe me; it took me a while to get used to Grant's proclivity towards dangerous activities."

God, how did she stand it?

It had taken every ounce of self-control to let Brian ride off with Grant this morning. "Have you ever asked Grant not to do something risky?" Riley gave voice to something she'd give serious consideration to doing. Knowing how Brian felt about the women in his life hovering, she'd kept her worries to herself.

Abby shook her head. "No. I trust him to be careful."

For Riley things weren't so simple. From experience she knew the most innocuous of events could turn deadly. She shook her head, pulling her thoughts out of that tailspin. Stewing about the dangers wasn't going to keep him safe or make him return any sooner. "I like the dress you picked out. It really shows off the work you've been doing in the gym."

"I can't wait to see Brian's expression when he sees you in the one you bought. He's going to be glad he agreed…" Her words trailed off as she turned her head towards the sound Riley had also caught. "I hear them coming."

She let out a breath, sagging into the seat. "I was hoping that wasn't my imagination."

A few minutes later two large motorcycles roared into Abby's driveway. *Holy cow!* Now that Brian had returned, she could appreciate the hotness that was her man astride the massive bike. She palmed her glass of iced tea, taking a sip.

After tugging off his helmet, he stalked over, pulling her in for a hard kiss. When he finally let her go, she was breathless and in need of more iced tea to cool off the desire coursing through her body. "I don't have to ask you if you had fun." He craved action like she did a good six-mile run. The sense of freedom couldn't easily be explained to those not addicted to the high from moving swiftly mile after mile. Brian had that look in his hazel eyes.

After saying quick goodbyes, he helped her into his low-slung car. "Where would you like to go to dinner?" He backed out of the driveway and heading towards Magnolia Springs.

She had half a mind to suggest skipping dinner in favor of going back to her place and making love for the next several hours. But he probably needed to eat. "How about we hit the food trucks over on Spring Street? I saw a write up about how the city was letting the owners use a vacant lot free of charge. The reporter said not only was the food great, but that the trucks were breathing new life into an older part of town."

He paused for a moment. "If that's what you want."

Worry ticked up a notch. He'd just said he'd eat anything that didn't eat him first, so it wasn't the eclectic cuisine. Before she had time to give more thought to what had his brow still furrowed, he placed his hand on her leg. His palm eased to indecent heights. "I hope you bought something pretty to show me later."

His touch stole her thoughts as it sent a charge of energy along her spine. As many times as he had hands on her, as often as he reached for her in the night, the contact still thrilled her. As did the way his hand automatically went to the small of her back once he'd helped her from the car. She loved not only the strength behind the gentle way he caressed her but also because in touching her, he showed the world she was his.

Riley leaned into his embrace, slipping her arm

around him as well. For someone as cast adrift as Riley had been most of her life, the feel of him acted like an anchor.

"You're thinking about it, aren't you?" He nuzzled her neck.

She shivered. "Remind me not to take up poker."

"I love what we do together." They walked towards the lot where the food trucks were parked entwined in each other.

"Me too." Last night, he'd made love to her until the aftereffects of her dream faded. "But I don't like being needy."

"You're the least needy person I know, but even with that it's okay to need someone." He caught her in his heated gaze.

The energy they shared was also becoming an addiction. "Let's eat quickly."

After buying half a dozen mouthwatering tacos from one truck and two bowls of interesting looking noodles from another, they headed towards the cluster of picnic tables at the far end of the lot. Now that Riley saw the location of the much-acclaimed mobile eateries, she knew what gave Brian a moment's pause. This wasn't the nicest part of Magnolia Springs.

"Why don't you take this side?" Brian pointed to the bench closest to the sidewalk, while he faced out. Not that he needed to remind her of his habit. Whether they were in a cozy café or an upscale restaurant, Brian always kept his wits about him and his eyes on the door.

Riley took a bit of her taco and scanned the area. While it wasn't The Avenucs of Wcst Magnolia, it certainly wasn't as bad as some of the Chicago neighborhoods she'd lived in back in the nineties. "Did you and Grant have a good time?"

Brian finished his fork full of noodles then wiped his mouth with a napkin. He might be one of the toughest men she'd ever known, but he also had the nicest manners. "It was fantastic. One of these days you and I will have to go out together." Excitement sparked in his hazel eyes.

Once in her life, she hadn't been afraid of anything, and if he were with her she might be that way again. "I'd like that. Maybe we can make a weekend of it."

"As soon as I get past the interview, we'll make some plans."

Riley tried to stay focused on what she had with him in this moment, not letting herself hope for what might happen once Brian no longer needed her to get the job. Talk of a future together ease the knot in her stomach she hadn't even realized was there.

A popping sound cut off her thoughts. The initial sound down the block was followed by two more. Just as her brain was processing the sound as gunfire, she was shoved to the ground. Gravel dug into her bare legs.

"Get your head down." Brian barked. Not waiting for her to comply, he forced her beneath him. Shouts and the sounds of people scrambling for cover were drowned out by her blood thrumming in her ears. Clinging to Brian, she prayed the violence down the street would stay there.

Within seconds sirens filled the air and Riley took a breath. She'd worried Brian would feel the need to head into the fray and was relieved beyond words that he'd stayed with her. As she eased off the ground, his vacant stare stole her relief.

"Brian, it's done. The cops are on their way." She grasped his chin and stared into his eyes. His pupils were dilated to the point she could barely make out their color.

When he didn't respond, she shook him. "You're with me here in Magnolia Springs."

Her pulse kicked into overdrive. "I need you to help me. You're on top of me and I think I may have twisted my leg." She hoped giving him something to do would snap him out of hell.

Immediately he rolled off her and began running his hands over her body. "Where does it hurt?"

"Just my knee." Maybe her diversion tactic wasn't a good one. "I'm fine. Just let me get up."

"Be still, dammit."

She gave in, lying passively while he went through the medic routine. "If we're going to play doctor, we probably should wait till we get home."

His glare told her he wasn't in the mood for her smart mouth. Finally, he helped her back to the picnic bench.

Riley looked around the open lot. Most of the patrons had returned to their seats and no one seemed to have noticed the drama that unfolded at their table, probably because they'd been too caught up in their own. Then she turned back to Brian, who rested his forearms on his legs. His head hung, making her regret so much that had happened in the past few minutes.

See, even the simplest of choices could turn ugly.

"Do you want to go?"

Brian lifted his head, his eyes no longer vacant, but haunted. "Is Barbie's ass plastic?" He bolted from his seat. Snagging Riley's hand, he practically dragged her up the sidewalk to his car. As he closed the door, his gaze turned towards the blue lights flashing up the street.

Other than the white-knuckle grip he had on the steering wheel, a casual observer might have thought nothing was amiss. He drove with his same carefulness, even reaching down to pat her hand when she placed it on his thigh. No one hid pain behind a mask better than Brian Stone. Riley let him have his space, hoping by the time they got home he'd be ready to talk.

Once they got back to her place he found her first-aid kit and tended to her scrapes, without a word. The silence made the air too heavy to breathe. By the time he stowed the kit in the bathroom and came to sit on the bed next to her, she'd had enough. She opened her mouth but bit back her words as he spoke.

"I'm so sorry I hurt you like that." The regret and self-recrimination on his face spoke of more than the few abrasions she'd gotten. Every dark event in his life seemed etched on his face at that moment.

Her soul ached to take away his pain. "What, this little scrape? You were looking out for me."

He looked away. "Not very well it would seem."

Riley planted her fists on her hips. "You think that I'm the only one in this relationship allowed to lose their shit. What about you telling me I had to wake you up when I had a nightmare, does that whole I've got your back thing only go one way?"

Several heartbeats of silence had Riley wondering if she'd pushed too hard. Finally, he lifted his chin, revealing pain etched on his face. "After all you've been through my issues are the last thing you should have to deal with."

If the two of them had any chance of making things work, he needed to let her carry her share of the load. "I want to be there for you." Rile took his hand. "Who else is going to understand?"

Brian shook his head. "My past is ugly. Even I don't like to go there. Why should you want to?"

Riley gave serious consideration to screaming. "So, let me get this straight." Her voice took on an edge as her temper got the better of her. "You're supposed to be there when I go off the deep end, but I can't return the favor. I don't know if that makes you a Neanderthal or an idiot."

"I don't like being weak." He gestured to his legs. "Don't you think this is enough for you to deal with? I don't want you to see me as an invalid." His lips formed a thin line, communicating clearly he'd talked things out as much as he planned to.

That was all fine and good. He could just listen for a minute. "Dammit, Brian Stone, you're twice the male of any man I know. Losing your legs only evened the playing field for those other guys."

The corners of his mouth twitched. "You're full of shit."

"So are you, if you think the way you reacted tonight makes you any less of a man. You protected me."

"Some protection I was." He folded his arms across his chest.

Riley wanted to shake him until his eyes rolled up in the back of his head. "You are the most hard-headed man on thc planct. What, I'm not supposed to be there for the man I love?"

His chin jerked up and the grin forming cooled her anger. "Well, I love you too, sunshine. Now come up here and let me show you how much." He tugged her down to the bed then pressed a kiss to the scrape on her elbow and the one on her knee. "So, you love me, huh."

She hadn't meant for that to leak out her mouth. "Swear to me that if that ever happens again you won't pull away."

"I swear." He studied her, the silence between them now sweet with the promise he'd made. "You have the most beautiful eyes I've ever seen. Next time I lose my shit, I'm going to lock onto your face and know immediately nothing as beautiful as your eyes could ever exist in hell."

Chapter Fourteen

Three weeks after the convenience store hold-up, the cops were still looking for the suspects, but that was the last thing on Brian's mind as he sat for his interview with Mobletech.

"Colonel Stone, tell us why you think you're the best candidate for this job."

He kept his expression an impassive mask though inwardly he smiled. The question posed must be in every management handbook because he'd been asked it at every interview he'd had since leaving the military. The lead interviewer, who'd introduced himself as Robert Nichols, flipped a page of the notebook he held in his lap. Two men flanked him, a thirty-something named Sam Ward, and Brian's contact from their army days, Daniel Weston, took turns posing questions during the hour-long interview.

Brian shifted in his seat. They'd already covered every job he'd had since receiving his commission as a lieutenant. After discussing his leadership style, he also disclosed as much of his last deployment to Afghanistan as he could. There were some aspects of his duties which would remain classified for at least another decade.

Briefly, he considered showing off his prosthetics as a literal demonstration of the lengths to which he would go to fulfill his duties, but dismissed the idea in case they might misinterpret it as a play on their emotions. He would earn this position because he was the most qualified, regardless of whether his legs were made of flesh and bone or metal and plastic.

He met Nichols's "I'm the best candidate because I don't give up when a situation proves harder than expected." His thoughts turned to the men he'd lost when that IED exploded underneath his Humvee. "And I take seriously my responsibility to those under my supervision." Though the job was for an instructor, making contractors field-ready could still prove to make the difference between life and death.

Nichols made a note on his paper. "Very good." He turned first to Colonel Weston then to Mr. Ward. "Do either of you have any further questions?"

The two men shook their head. The question left unasked was how his injury would affect his ability to train Mobletech operatives, especially when they left the classroom for field exercises. It wouldn't—and he had Riley to thank for that. "Thank you, gentlemen for the chance to interview with you." He shook each man's hand in turn.

Weston followed him into the hall. "You nailed the interview, Stone. Only one other applicant has come close to giving the answers you have."

"That's good to hear." All he had to do now was pass the physical fitness part of the interview.

Weston pointed to his right. "If you follow this hallway, you'll find a locker room where you can change for the test."

Following the directions, Brian set his gym bag on a bench. After shedding his suit and hanging it in one of the lockers, he fished out a pair of nylon track pants from his bag. The Mobletech people knew about his injury, but there was no sense in reminding them. He pulled on the long pants and was lacing his shoes when a voice from behind stopped him.

"I'll be damned if it isn't Brainstorm. What are you doing here?"

Annoyance racked through him at the sound of the guy's overly friendly greeting. Major Tom Payne was a slippery bastard who spent his military career kissing ass. He'd also shake with one hand while stabbing you in the back with the other.

Brian hid his irritation and went for the short-but-sweet response. "I'm interviewing for a position." He noted the guy's sweat soaked t-shirt. "Same as you from the looks of things."

Payne puffed out his chest. "Yeah, I blew them out of the water on the interview then aced my physical fitness test. Did the run in eighteen-thirty." The corner of his mouth curled in an arrogant sneer. "I didn't think they made the desk jockeys pass the P.T. exam."

"They don't." Brian made quick work of tying his other shoe. He stood, needing to get the hell out of the locker room. There was only so much bull he could take and Payne had reached that limit years ago.

"Good luck, B.S. You ought to be proud of yourself for trying, no matter how things play out."

He ignored Payne's bating and grabbed his water bottle and a towel. "They're expecting me in the gym. Better not keep them waiting." Following the wall placards, he found the employees' gym. He drew in a breath and pushed open the swinging doors. The large room was like any number of workout rooms he'd been in. A row of treadmills lined one wall, with weight machines in the middle and an open area with mats on the floor.

The only person in the room was a young woman, probably in her early thirties. Dressed in workout gear and holding a clipboard, she motioned to him. As he approached she extended her hand. "I'm Amy. I run the gym Mobletech has for their employees and will be administering your exam."

Though so much rode on his performance during the next few minutes, the uptick in his pulse came more from anticipation than anxiety. All military personnel took a yearly physical fitness test and repeating a task he'd done so many times felt like another step in the right toward his goal of reclaiming parts of his life that he'd lost.

While she reminded him that he needed to do a minimum of fifty-nine push-ups and sit-ups in two minute sessions, and run two miles in under eighteen minutes, forty-two seconds, his thoughts were on the person who'd helped him get to this moment. Sure, he might have done this on his own, but Riley's not-always-gentle prodding changed more than his BMI. He needed to find some way to show her how much he appreciated her efforts. And the growing love he had for her.

"Where would you like to begin?"

"Let's start with sit-ups." He dropped Crossing his arms over his chest, he waited for her signal. Sit-ups were the easiest of the three, given they put the least amount of strain on his stumps. He kept count in his head as he brought his chest to his thighs then let his head touch the mat. The first ten were merely a warmup, and it wasn't until he reached the thirty that his abs began to burn. He powered on, and reaching the magic number added fuel to his efforts so that when she called "time" he'd completed seventy-two.

She marked his score on her clipboard. "You can take a moment to stretch if you like."

Brian took the woman up on her offer then he wiped the sweat from his face with a towel before taking a sip from his water bottle. With that, he dropped back to the mat. Push-ups were more of a challenge since they put pressure on his feet as well as the artificial socket that acted as his knee. He made his body a level plane with his elbows locked. At her signal, he lowered himself until his nose touched the mat. Keeping his body level, he kept count as he had with the sit-ups. Thirty push-ups in, the real work began. Sweat trickled down his face and into his eyes. Ignoring the burn in both his eyes and his shoulders which were screaming, he powered passed the required sixty push-ups. At the two-minute mark, Brian dropped to his stomach.

"Seventy." She confirmed his count. He sat up, jerking his chin in acknowledgement. Not bad for an old man. He took a second to congratulate himself on acing two out of the three components.

As he took another sip of water, he noticed Major Payne and Colonel Weston stood just inside the gym. Brian tuned out his audience. Regardless of whether they were there to root him on or anxious to see him trip and go sliding off the end of the treadmill, his only competition was himself, his only adversary doubt.

He mounted the treadmill and punched the Power button. Beginning in his usual steady jog, the half-mile mark came and went with only the increase in his heart rate and breathing. At the one-mile mark, he really began to feel where his knee had contacted the ground last week. The socket of his prosthetic limb rubbed painfully against his stump and he was sure when he got home tonight he'd find a lovely blister. He wiped the pain from his thoughts. He'd had much worse than the irritation he was experiencing. In the past he also hadn't had something as wonderful to look forward to at the end of the day.

He wanted Riley to be proud of him and pleased she'd decided to take him on—not only as a client but as a lover as well. Recalling how the drill sergeants from basic training had sung ditties while the soldiers ran, Brian sang a cadence about a young girl—substituting Riley's name for Jane's. Though both knees ached like a son-of-a-bitch and he could feel blood trickling from his stump, he dug deep and increased his pace. He wasn't going to simply finish the two miles; he was going to do it faster than ever before. He let his mind travel away from the continuous pounding of his feet against the treadmill, instead imaging himself and Riley running through the streets around her home as they had so many times in the past few weeks.

Amy's call of "time" brought him from his inner monologue. He hit the Power button and stepped off the end of the treadmill. Planting his palms against his thighs, he breathed deeply though lungs that had turned to concrete. Someone passed him a towel, which he used to wipe the sweat from his eyes.

"Fourteen minutes, eight seconds."

He wanted to crow. A personal best by almost thirty seconds. He couldn't wait to see the broad smile on Riley's face, but for now he'd enjoy the expressions of those in the room. While Amy and Weston's congratulatory smiles were appreciated, the look of disappointment on Payne's face before he turned on his heels and left the gym had Brian biting the inside of his cheek to keep from laughing.

Weston patted him on the back. "Damn, B.S, I thought you were going to burn up the motor on that treadmill."

He shrugged. "Just another jog through the park. You look happier with my performance than I am."

The colonel's eyes cut to the swinging doors. "Let's just say, I'm relieved to see the best man can still come out on top once in a while." He gripped Brian's shoulder. "When can you start?"

****

"*Happy birthday to you* . . . ."

Riley sang along with her fellow employees, her mind far from the people gathered around Davis Air Transport's conference table. Brian was in Arizona for his interview and PT test with Mobletech. The wait was killing her. Had she done enough to help him? Pulling her lips into a smile, she turned her attention to the people in the room.

As the song died amid cheers and laughter, she shot a glance to her right at the recipient of the song. A bright flush turned Truck's round jowly face florid.

"You shouldn't have, really." He echoed a sentiment she shared. His reluctance didn't keep the man from grinning broadly as he sliced off huge chunks of chocolate cake. "Just you wait, your turn is coming." He past her a piece.

"That's what I'm afraid of." She made a mental

note to be absent the last Friday in October.

At the head of the table, Grant stood. "Before we head back to work. I want to take a second to recognize an anniversary of sorts." His eyes shot to her. "Six months ago, Riley Logan joined the Davis Air Transport family, and I have to say she's made more improvements than to just our accountant's life."

Her attention was drawn to Maggie as she brought up a small gift bag. "We wanted to say thanks. For everything." The sparkle in the woman's eye touched a chord in Riley. Not only had she accepted that Brian and Riley were dating, but she also embraced it with vigor.

Riley pulled a coffee mug from the bag that read *World's Best Friend.*

"Speech," someone down the table yelled.

"Yeah, like that's going to happen." For someone who had always wanted to belong, she didn't know what to do with it when she got it. She gripped the table. "Thanks, y'all." She used the southern pronoun that once seemed corny and now was second nature. "If I'd known how great it was to live in the south, I'd have come here sooner."

As soon as was polite, she returned to her desk. Her mind swirled everywhere but on accounts receivable.

"When is Brian getting back from Tucson?" Maggie asked.

She looked up from her computer. "His flight lands at six tonight."

"Have him call me. I want to hear how it went."

"Sure, no problem."

Something inside Riley had eased in the weeks

since they'd exchanged the three little words. There was no longer any doubt of whether he would be at her house when she got home. If he didn't have uncle duty, she'd find him on the treadmill when she walked in at the end of the day.

She'd have Brian call his sister once she was finished with him. Certain he'd do well on the interview, she'd made plans for them to celebrate when he got back. She'd even bought a sexy night gown. She clenched her eyes to stop her thoughts from running away with her. If she didn't get a grip on her imagination, she'd be stuck at her desk all night.

Minutes later, Riley was once again pulled from her half-hearted attempts at working. "When's our boy getting back?" Grant asked.

"In two hours, fifteen minutes."

He barked a laugh. "Not that you're keeping track or anything."

"I've got my reputation as a personal trainer riding on how his PT test went."

He propped a hip on the edge of her desk. "You've done more for him than just getting his broken ass back in fighting shape."

Riley didn't know what to do with so much gratitude. These people had saved her sanity, making her feel rooted when she'd felt she could blow away and never be missed. Her chest tightened thinking about Brian. Like one battle wary survivor to another, he'd seen where she'd been without her having to explain. Falling in love with him had been the most unexpected, most natural thing she'd ever done. Words failed her. How could she explain what he had come to mean to her? Or the fear she still felt when she thought of what his job might do to change what she'd come to hold so dear. "I…" She looked at her boss.

He rolled his eyes. "Look at me. See what marriage does to a guy." He gripped her shoulder. "I just wanted to say thanks. If Heather tries to lure you away, let me make you a better offer."

The woman had made Riley a couple offers which she'd politely turned down. "I will."

Grant turned to leave then made a one-eighty. "Before I forget, Abby said she wants the four of us to have dinner one night soon."

"I'll check with Brian and have him get back to you."

He winked. "I'm hoping you guys will have other things to talk about, so just let me know when you can. And on that note, why don't you bug out of here a little early." He pointed to the files on her desk. "I'm sure no little accounting elves are going to slip in here tonight and do it for you."

A couple hours later, Riley wasn't so sure Grant had the right idea. Roaming around her house only served to make her more nervous rather than less. When six o'clock came and went and she hadn't heard from Brian, her anxiety began to get the better of her. She debated calling Maggie to see if he'd gone there instead. At eight she forced herself to sit. It was that or wear a pattern in the carpet. She flicked on the T.V. hoping for a distraction.

When her cell phone went off, she had it to her ear before it rang twice. "What's up?" She really wanted to ask if he was okay.

"Still here in Tucson. Our plane left the gate, but the tower won't let us take off because of a thunderstorm. We're stuck on the taxiway. I'm not supposed to have my phone out, so I better hang up before they catch me. I just didn't want you to worry."

Riley's anxiety ratcheted down, but only a notch. She worked in the aviation field and knew how safety conscious everyone was, that still didn't settle a nagging feeling of dread at the base of her spine. "Call me when you land. I don't care how late it is."

Grant's words echoed in her ears. How had Brian come to mean so much to her in such a short period of time? She turned her attention to the T.V. where one of those reality wedding shows played. She never watched shows like that, didn't see the appeal in the forced drama. This bride said caught her attention. She zeroed in on the woman in the puffy white confection.

"My fiancé was one of my first husband's army buddies. After Drew was killed in action, Brett started checking on me. The romance blossomed after that. We just want our dream wedding before he's deployed again."

Riley leaned forward. "Is she crazy?"

Having lost a policeman husband in the line of duty, she couldn't imagine marrying another cop. She snapped off the T.V. and snagged her e-reader. Thank God, Brian's job wouldn't take him back to another war zone.

****

Brian used his key to let himself into Riley's house. Without turning on the lights, he slipped down the hall. A beam of light from the bathroom cast a light on her sleeping form, stopping him where he stood. The decision he hadn't thought twice about hours ago suddenly didn't seem so obvious considering what met him. God, she was beautiful. With her dark hair spilling across the pillow, he couldn't imagine giving this up for a job. A fucking desk job at that.

Knowing how much Riley needed the connections she'd formed here in Magnolia Springs, he couldn't ask her to follow him to Tucson. Yet. Hopefully, she'd be willing to put up with a long-distance relationship until they figured out a better plan.

After stripping down to his boxers, he slipped into her bed to find her covered in the silkiest fabric he'd ever touched. Brian peeled back the covers. Ivory. Satin. Negligee. He shook his head. Something that sensuous should be illegal. His gaze coasted over her body, pausing to take in the peaks of her nipples pressing through the bodice of the ivory gown.

Riley stirred. "How'd it go?" She curled into his body.

"Two miles in fourteen minutes, eight seconds." His hand slid further south. "I smoked the competition."

"I'm so proud of you."

That wasn't the emotion he wanted most from her. He drew her closer, tucking her head under his chin. He was about to test the tentative bonds they'd built over the last couple weeks. But all that could keep. Tonight, they knew where they stood with each other. Tomorrow would be soon enough to worry about the future.

"I missed you today."

His hand tunneled beneath her nightgown to caress her long, lean back. Compared to her skin, the negligee was like burlap. Even half asleep, the way she arched into him as his hands trailed over the peaks and valleys of her body made him wild with need. Her sensuality wasn't the only thing that had his heart beating out a tattoo. Her willingness to take a chance on love again blew him away. "I missed you, too."

The words didn't convey everything he felt for her so he kissed her instead. Hard. He threw everything he had into that kiss hoping she'd somehow know. "Let me show you how much I missed you."

Brian did. For hours. Until they collapsed into a tangle of arm and legs and slept. Sometime later, the smell of coffee teased him from his dream. It had been a good one, with him and Riley on a beach somewhere.

The next morning, he woke when she entered the bedroom already dressed in workout gear. "You went for a run without me." Sweat glistened on her skin, reminding him of the first time he'd seen her. Only now he was free to act on the driving urge to taste the salty droplets. He took the mug of coffee from her then tugged her on top of him. Brian nibbled the slender column of her neck, making her squeal in a very un-Riley-like display of effervescence.

She peered up from a fringe of dark lashes. "I didn't wake you because I figured you were due a day off after yesterday's stellar performance."

He rolled them over, using his forearms to keep from putting too much weight on her. "How about a repeat of last night's performance?"

Riley shook her head. "After you tell me how the interview went."

He had been waiting until the perfect moment to give something to her. He'd seen it in a jewelry store he'd passed when the colonel took him to lunch. It was crazy considering everything she'd said pointed to her not being ready for anything more than what they had.

He needed to give her something tangible, a way of

her knowing she belonged to him. "First, I brought you back something." He grabbed the computer bag he'd left at the side of the bed. His hand shook as he palmed the black velvet box.

"You didn't have to bring me anything. Seeing you this stoked is all the thanks I need."

"This isn't a thank you gift."

God hadn't made a rock big enough to even out the scales for what she'd done for him. More than helping him get back in physical shape, she'd give him a purpose beyond getting through the day. Brian held out the jewelry box. Her gaze widened. "It's not what you think. I know you're not ready for that." He cracked open the lid, turning it so she could see the necklace.

She touched the stones with her fingertips. "It's gorgeous."

"It's only fitting a beautiful woman wear something equally beautiful. Although now that I have a side-by-side comparison, I see your eyes are a little bluer than these amethysts. Perhaps I should have gotten the Tanzanites instead."

After turning around Riley held her long hair out of the way so he could fasten the clasp then she walked to the dresser, fingering the necklace in front of the mirror.

Brian slipped behind her, wrapping his arms around her. "I'm beginning to think I should have bought you a pair of cowboy boots."

"No. I love it."

"But…"

She eyed him in the mirror. "You said you knew I wasn't ready for a ring. Does that mean you are?"

He kissed the top of her head. "Rings, necklaces,

matching motorcycles, I want you to know how serious I am about the two of us making this work."

It was several minutes before they did anymore talking. He was much better at letting his lips, tongue, and hands do the communicating. Eventually, he ran out of stalling tactics. With one final kiss he dove in. "They offered me the instructor job."

Riley ran her fingers through his hair, soothing him. "I'm not surprised."

"See, here's the deal." He tilted her chin, needing to see her eyes. "Remember a few weeks ago we watched a news report on Al Qaeda's activity in South America? I'll be preparing contractors who'll travel to Argentina, Bolivia, and Paraguay to monitor the situation."

"But you're not going to be doing anything dangerous, right?" Her voice climbed several octaves.

He ran a thumb over her cheek. "I'll take the contractors on field exercises here in the states, but that's not any riskier than a camping trip."

"That's great." She relaxed in his arms. "You're a great leader and I know Mobletech will be glad to have you pass along your expertise."

"So, you're okay with me taking the job?"

Riley nodded. "Absolutely, I work for a company that specializes in getting people and things across long distances. I imagine you could convince Grant to let you hitch a ride home now and then."

He buried his face in her hair. "You're something else." He was the luckiest bastard on the planet to have a woman like her.

"I could also come visit you, if you like."

"You better." He was ten pounds lighter with that

worry off his back.

"That settles it," she said, moving from his embrace. "I think we should celebrate."

Brian pulled her back. "I know what I'd like to do."

"There's that but I also think it would be a good idea to have a cookout here."

"You'd want to do that. I know crowds aren't your thing."

She nodded. "Absolutely. We have lots to celebrate."

Chapter Fifteen

Heat stole Riley's breath as she stepped from her kitchen to the deck. A barbeque had seemed like a good idea when she'd suggested it to Brian two weeks ago. Now, she wasn't so sure. Brian assured her come the middle of September the temperatures would cool off a bit, but she hadn't wanted to wait another month to celebrate her guy's good news. Besides, he'd be out in Arizona by then.

She set the bowl of chips and salsa on the patio table she'd bought at an end-of-the-season sale. "Can I get anyone another beer?"

Besides Grant and Abby's son, Jack, Riley invited the Victory for Veterans volunteers plus a few of Brian's high school classmates. Twenty people showed up, most making use of her shaded back yard. Several of the guys joined Brian in manning the grill she'd also bought when they purchased the patio furniture.

Brian tugged her onto his lap. "We're fine, baby. Relax. Everyone's having a great time."

Despite his assurance, she scanned her back yard seeing if her guests needed anything. The oak trees dotting her back yard provided plenty of cool shade. As she and Brian put the swing together, she'd envisioned lots of warm summer evenings the two of them cozied together on it.

As much as she'd have like to take a breather, she

171

couldn't let herself give into the nausea that had woken her that morning or the fatigue plaguing her the last week. Besides, Brian was hot, and not just the panty melting hotness that he usually was. It had to be nearly ninety degrees on the deck, making her think it might be possible to cook the meat without the benefit of charcoal.

She wiggled out of Brian's arms to adjust the umbrella so that it blocked some of the late afternoon sun.

"Let me do that." He adjusted the umbrella's angle. "You're doing too much."

Riley smiled, enjoying the little kindnesses he showed her. His treatment bordered on spoiling. She hadn't opened a car door or hauled in groceries in weeks. Once they stepped inside her gym, things were different. It was all about the competition there, and that was enough to keep her inner feminist satisfied. "It's not too much. I want your family and friends to have a good time."

A dark look crossed his expression and Brian turned to the guys behind him. "Fend for yourselves a minute. Something needs my attention for a minute."

"They're your friends now as much as they are mine." He fixed her with a stare. "Maggie and the kids can also be your family."

Riley responded to his hint by planting a chase kiss on his cheek. She was no longer looking from the outside, wishing for what other's had. Her heart was too full and the English language, never her friend under the best of scenarios, seemed inadequate to express her feelings.

"When you're ready." His brows knitted. "Go sit

down and enjoy your guests."

Riley wiggled out of his embrace. "I will in a minute. I need to get a few more burgers on the grill."

"Grilling is my manly duty."

"Manly duty. Where's it written that by virtue of your anatomy you're supposed the cook the meat?"

"It's the first commandment in the caveman handbook. Thou shalt offer burnt sacrifice upon the open flame." Brian followed up his response with a series of grunts.

"You win. Far be it from me to cause you to break a commandment." She eyed the shady yard below. "I'll go sit with Abby. The two of us can compare notes on who has the most trying male."

I am one lucky son-of-a-gun.

Brian had a job that while he wasn't in love with, it was one where he could give her some of the things Riley deserved. Most importantly, they had each other, and hopefully soon he could convince her to marry him. Seeing how she'd accepted the amethyst necklace, gave him hope she'd react similarly when he gave her the engagement ring he'd also bought.

"You sure you want to take a job that keeps you away from her?" Grant tapped into one of his concerns.

"Not in the least. I wish something had worked out a little closer to home." As unexciting as Mobletech would be, it was better than loafing around like he had since retiring from the army. Although he had to admit playing manny to Lexi and Matt had been awesome.

Grant nodded in the direction of the back yard. "Not that I'm trying to get rid of her, but do you think Riley would consider joining you?"

Brian shrugged. He hadn't asked, knowing how

important it was for her to put down roots. "Maybe in the future. She'd not ready now. Besides, I'll be working long hours for a few months trying to get this program up to speed. It wouldn't be fair to ask her to move out and then leave her alone for days on end."

"You want some unsolicited advice, my man?"

Brian rolled his eyes. "Do I have a choice?"

"No," I really fucked things up with Heather by working crazy hours. Don't make that same mistake."

Easy for him to say. "Well, we can't all be millionaires." Twenty years in the army hadn't made Brian a rich man. While he was far from broke, he wanted to offer Riley something when they finally started their lives together as a married couple.

"The saying's true, you can't buy happiness."

Brian had been letting an idea marinate in the back of his mind. He didn't want millions, just enough to buy a place for Riley. At his rate of pay, it would take at least a couple years for a down payment.

Before he had the chance to run this idea past Grant, his phone went off. Pulling it from his hip pocket, he saw the Tucson area code. "I better get this." He stepped to Riley's living room, his gut telling him this wasn't an ordinary phone call. "What's up, Colonel? Don't tell me shit's getting critical already."

The man chuckled. "How do you feel about trading the dry heat of Arizona for jungle heat?"

Brian's pulse kicked into gear. *Hell yeah.* "I hear it's good for the complexion."

When he hung up a few minutes later he'd been offered an obscene amount of money, enough to buy Riley anything she wanted. A grin formed on his face. Brian couldn't remember the last time he'd been this stoked. Sure, there was an element of danger involved, but that just made the job that much better.

Riley crossed the yard, checking in with each of her guest before sitting next to Abby on the swing. "Having a good time?"

"The best." Abby patted her knee. "I'm so happy for Brian."

"He's really excited about the job. He worked really hard to get this position and he's definitely earned a second chance."

Abby turned to face Riley. "I'm not just talking about the job. I'm happy he's found someone who makes him happy."

She ducked her chin. "Thanks." Guilt no longer plagued her like it had when she first met Brian. Jake would have like Brian and have wanted her to have a life after he died. Still, anxiety whispered in the background, like the soundtrack of a movie warning the viewer of impending trouble. "Let me freshen your drink." She took Abby's glass, using the good hostess routine to distract herself.

Once inside her air-conditioned kitchen Riley drew in a deep breath, enjoying not only the cool air, but the much-needed distraction. There wasn't any sense worrying about something that hadn't even happened. She still had her hands in the ice maker when her back door opened with a slam.

"Aunt Riley," Lexi cried.

Riley's heart skipped a beat at the honorarium as she bent down to little girl. "What's wrong?"

Lexi flung her arms around Riley's neck. "I got stung by a bee."

Riley hefted the little girl onto the counter and

brushed the hair from her face. "Where'd it get you?" With Maggie making a run to the store for more ice, Riley tried to guess how her friend would have handled the emergency. Not having much firsthand experience with kids, she went with calm and assured rather than being overly emotional and risk upsetting the girl even more.

Lexi pointed to her arm. "Grace and I were eating watermelon and it started flying around her. I shooed it away and it bit me."

Riley examined the whelp, looking for the stinger. There wasn't one, so there wasn't much more she could do but ease the pain. With one hand on the girl's knee, Riley reached for a couple ice cubes. "Does that feel better?"

"No." Her bottom lip trembled.

The look on the little girl's face tore at Riley's heart. *What parents went through, wasn't for sissies.* "You're being very brave and such a good friend to look after Grace."

Lexi looked up, her face becoming serious. "Uncle Brian says it's important to look after others, especially if they can't take care of themselves."

"Your uncle is right." It wasn't possible to love him more than she already did, but she with Lexi's proclamation, her love for him swelled.

As if her thoughts had conjured him up, he stepped from the living room into the kitchen. "What's all this crying about?" He ran a hand over Lexi's head, before pressing a kiss to Riley's temple.

"I think it was a yellow jacket. Is she allergic?"

Brian shook his head. "No."

Lexi tapped Brian on the arm. "It's feeling better

now. Can I go back outside?"

When he didn't offer his niece an answer, Riley turned to see what had so quickly distracted him. While he seemed to be gazing at something on the far side of her kitchen window, something told her it wasn't her crepe myrtle trees that had his attention.

"Sure." She helped Lexi down from the counter. When the door closed behind Lexi, she turned to him. "What's wrong?" Her heart pounded. Did she really want to know?

He pulled her into an embrace. "I just got some good news."

Riley opened her mouth to ask what that good news was at the same moment Grant stuck his head in the back door. "There's a party going on out here. You two can make out later."

With his arm still around Riley's waist, Brian followed his friend out onto the deck. Seeing their guests gathered congregated on Riley's large deck, he decided now was a good time to share his news.

"What's put that smile on your face, my brother? Besides the obvious."

If he waited another minute he'd explode. "Someone just made me an offer I can't refuse. In exchange for eleven months of my life, I can give my girl here the world."

Riley's eyes grew wide. "What do you mean?"

With the word of the conflict in the tri-border area not having been widely reported in the news and the American government wanting it that way, he had to word his answer carefully. "Uncle Sam might not want my broke ass, but it seems a South American country can make use of me." He turned to Riley, cupping her face in his palm. "And when I come back, I'm buying you the world."

Riley swayed and he had to grab her shoulders to hold her steady. "Are you okay, babe? You look like you're getting ready to faint."

She waved off his attention, side stepping his embrace. "I'm just over heated, that's all. I just need to sit down for a minute."

As he helped her to one of the chairs under the large umbrella, something told him the white-as-a-sheet look on her face wasn't due to the heat. His gut also told him Riley needed a minute to herself, so he took up a spot next to Grant along the deck's railing. Maybe his buddy had a better idea what to do.

"Is she okay?"

He shrugged. "She said she was fine." Thought for the past few days she hadn't been feeling well.

"I've seen that look before on Abby's face. It didn't turn out well."

Whether she needed her space or not, Brian couldn't let her sit there like that without checking on her. He knelt in front of her, trying not to draw the attention of the other guests who'd gone back to eating. No better than she liked attention, Riley would have his hide if he made a scene in front of her guests.

"What's wrong?"

She shook her head.

"Tell me."

Pain crossed her face before she hid it behind an impassive mask. "I can't, not now."

"Are you sick?"

"I'm fine." She turned away when he tried to touch

her forehead.

"I told you that you were doing too much."

She worked her jaw like she was trying not to lose her lunch. "I need a minute. Please see if anyone needs something."

Brian rejoined Grant along the deck railing. "I don't get it. She said she's fine, but clearly she's not."

Grant folded his arms across his chest. "I'm no expert on women, as the ones in my life will tell you, but I don't think you should have made the announcement without talking to Riley first."

"Why?"

Grant dismissed Brian's question with a wave. "Man, if you can't figure that out for yourself. You're screwed."

He was. He really was. "I really don't get it. This job is what I've been hoping for."

Grant shot a glance around at the other guests. "Let me see if I can get everyone out of here. You two need to talk." Then he clapped Brian on the shoulder. "I'll be rooting for you."

Still confused, Brian shot a look at his buddy. "Thanks, man. I think I'll need it."

Chapter Sixteen

Riley's stomach rolled, more a protest of the lies she'd swallowed than the charred food she'd recently eaten. She left the cluster of guests, feeling anything but the happy hostess. The ringing in her ears drowned out their questions. This just simply couldn't be happening. She clenched her eyes. *He'd promised.* Promised before they ever become lovers he wouldn't take a dangerous job. And she'd helped him get it. A dark thought flashed through her tormented mind. Had he lied to get what he wanted?

Sometime later Brian found her in the bedroom. "They're gone." He sat on the edge of the bed. "I told everyone you weren't feeling well."

At first all she could do was nod. Although "not feeling well" hardly explained what she was going through. "Thank you." She could barely get the two words past the strangle hold emotion had on her throat.

Brian took her hand. "Listen, I get that I screwed up. I should have talked to you first." Riley's gaze lifted to meet his. "Did you lie to me?" When his brows knit in confusion, she asked again. "Did you lie to me so I'd help you? Was it your intention on taking a job like this one the whole time?"

"No! Until an hour ago I thought I was going to Tucson."

A fraction of her tension eased. She believed him.

He was a lot of things, deceptive wasn't one of them. "I'm sorry. My mind is playing catch up."

"It's a lot to take in. Ask me anything about this new assignment and if it's not classified I'll tell you."

The hows and whens didn't matter. Not even the why of it all. "I have only one question. Do you have to take this assignment, or is the other one still on the table?"

"They want me for the South American job and I want to take it." He squeezed her hand. "God, Riley you have to know what this means to me. To be back in the action. To matter again. It would be almost like Afghanistan never happened."

She'd never heard so much passion in his voice. Her heart ached so much had been taken from him. He deserved to be happy, to do something that made him feel whole.

He brushed his fingers through her hair, a gesture he'd done so many times since they'd been together. It had always soothed her until tonight. Only one thing could put her world back together, for him not to go.

"When I get back. I'll have the money to buy you anything you want. Maybe you could start your own workout facility. Or we could buy a house together."

Riley blinked. After all she'd told him about herself, he thought for one second she cared about material things. Heat raced through her veins. "I'd rather rent a one-bedroom shack and know you were safe than have to endure a year's worth of terror."

He continued touching her hair. "Nothing's going to happen to me there. I'll always have two bodyguards with me. Mobletech and the U.S. government isn't going to let anything happen to me."

She shook her head. "You can't make those kinds of guarantees. Weren't you with an escort when that roadside bomb went off?"

"Baby, lightening doesn't strike twice in the same place."

Brian tried wrapping her in his arms, but Riley fought against his embrace. "Do you think I'm that stupid or are you being that naive?"

The Bridal show she'd watched the other week popped into her head. That bride must have been thinking the same thing. She wasn't that optimistic. "You can't seriously believe there's some cosmic quota for tragedy and once it's reached a person is exempt from further heartbreak." Sarcasm infused her words. It was that or scream, yell, and pound her fists against his chest to get him to listen.

Brian made a grab for her, pulling her into his lap. "I think the universe owes the two of us some happiness."

She barked a laugh. "The universe isn't that fair minded."

"Can't you believe in the two of us, that I'd do anything to come back to you?"

Riley thought of all the hours she'd spent waiting for Jake to come home after a shift. How the sound of his tires on the driveway had seemed like music. The relief at knowing they'd been granted another day together had been heaven after hours of purgatory. "I can't. I can only believe in what I can see with my own two eyes and feel with my hands. Simply hoping doesn't make it so."

Brian stiffened beneath her. "I need this job."

Riley chuffed. "Funny." Though nothing of this

struck her as humorous. "I remember you saying the same thing about me."

"You do. You mean the world to me."

"Just not as much as chasing after an adventure."

Brian's jaw got tight. "Don't make me choose."

"I can't smile and wave the flag." No matter unpatriotic it made her sound. "This isn't even our country we're talking about."

"Don't these people deserve peace?" His gaze heated.

"Don't I?"

Brian stood. "I know I've dumped a lot on you. We'll talk about this again after you've had a couple days to let this sink in."

Riley rounded on him. "Time isn't going to change anything and talking won't change my mind." They didn't have a failure to communicate. They had a failure to be right for each other. He needed someone who could let him be who he was and she needed someone who'd come home at the end of the day. "If you go, I can't be the one waiting at home for you."

"Pushing me away won't keep me from getting hurt."

She clenched her eyelids to block out the image of his broken body lying in some Godforsaken jungle. "I know that, but at least I don't have to be there to watch."

"I can't believe you're giving me this ultimatum." Pain turned his voice to gravel.

Riley raised her head to look him in the eye. He needed to see the seriousness of her words. "When Jake was killed, part of me died as well. I loved Jake practically my whole life. He was the only one who knew everything I'd been through. He was my sunshine. As much as I loved him, I love *you* a thousand times more. You understand all those dark places inside me. I'd never survive losing you to something as senseless as war. A war that you've chased down to be part of."

Her heart ached as it pounded in her chest. "This isn't an ultimatum as you called it and I'm not trying to call your bluff. You have every right to know where I stand on this. Just like you have every right to make your own choices."

Heat radiated from his eyes. "I guess we should call it a night."

"Perhaps we should. I know neither of us wants to say hurtful things we don't mean." Riley walked into the bathroom, unable to watch him leave. She'd already hurt him so much.

****

Brian brought his car to a stop in Maggie's driveway. On the drive over all the anger that caused him to storm out of Riley's evaporated, leaving him drained, dazed, and dumb. Had he lost the only woman he'd ever loved to take the only job he'd ever wanted? Pain tightened his chest until he could hardly breathe. After several deep breaths, he finally released the death grip he had on the steering wheel, going through the motions of turning off the car's engine with the same auto-pilot movements that brought him home.

What the fuck just happened? He shook his head, trying to stop the ringing in his ears. Unfortunately, this wasn't the first time he'd experienced this numb all over sensation. Or having the mundane go south on him. He was shell shocked, just like right after that EID had exploded underneath him. The only difference this time was at least the casualties of this cluster fuck were limited to two.

Several minutes later he was still frozen behind the wheel. As the numbness wore off, reality began setting up shop in his gut. He'd blown it with Riley, big time. Maybe for good. Shaking himself loose from the threads of angst, he opened the car door. He wasn't ready to admit defeat just yet. She just needed time to get used to the idea of him going to South America for the year.

She wasn't the only one not ready to face some things. He wasn't ready for an inquisition from his sister. She'd returned from her errand in time for his announcement and had left with the other guests when he said Riley had gotten sick. Moving commando quiet, he slipped through the family room hoping not to wake his family.

"What are you doing here?" Maggie asked from the darkness of the family room.

Brian jerked his attention to the sofa. With his mind only scene he'd left back a Riley's he'd failed to notice the glow from Maggie's laptop. "I live her, don't I?"

Maggie closed the lid on her laptop, placing it on the coffee table. "Well, yeah. You used to at least. I would have thought you and Riley would be celebrating your good news."

"Change of plans." He quickened his progress through the family room.

Her brows drew together. "What happened?" She patted the seat next to her. "Tell me about it."

Brian clenched his fist. A part of him wanted to

lash out at Maggie, to focus on her mother-hen tendencies instead of real problem at hand. Instead, he sucked back the anger that lit up his insides. She didn't deserve the wrath and he had about as much chance as a snowball in hell of figuring this out for himself.

Brian's head slumped. "Riley doesn't want to see me anymore."

"Why, what did you do?" She sat up.

"Took that job." He dropped to the sofa. "She said she couldn't sit around at home waiting for a phone call telling her I was dead."

Maggie snagged his hand, giving it a squeeze. "Just give her some time to adjust to the news. You'll see. She'll come around. She just doesn't understand what military life's like."

Brian wasn't so sure that was the case. Riley wasn't one who said things she didn't mean or exaggerate to make a point. He shook his head. "Somehow, I get the feeling she understands all too well. Her husband was a cop, after all."

Her words pinged around in Brian's skull, his thoughts latching onto one thing. She loved him more than she loved her husband. How could that be? How could she love him and then push him away? He had no frame of reference when it came to her fears of losing a loved one. Death was a part of life and no one was guaranteed anything more than the moment he stood in.

"Would you like me to talk to her? I could let her know she's not alone in this."

He was desperate enough to accept any help. "That be great." With that he wandered back to his bedroom, hoping when he woke in the morning he'd find the last couple hours had all been a nightmare.

****

The heavy metal door leading from the hangar groaned on its hinges. One more time, Riley's head popped over the top of her cubical at the sound, hoping it signaled Maggie's arrival. With the exchange of heated words between Riley and Brian still banging around in her head, she was desperate to talk to her friend. Surely if anyone could get him to listen, it would be his sister.

At the sight of one of Davis Air Transport's mechanics, Riley slumped back into her seat. Within seconds she was back to peeling at the already thinned layer of nails. If Maggie didn't get to work soon, she might have only bloody nubs with which to input the company's accounts.

Ordinarily, she wouldn't have involved a third party in her problems, especially since Maggie was both Riley's friend as well as Brian's sister. She was desperate though, as well as grateful to have someone she could confide in. When the door groaned again, Riley was out of her seat like one of those moles at a carnival game. The sight of Maggie's auburn hair sent Riley's hopes flying and she rounded the walls of her cubical racing for Maggie like she was a lifeline.

"Can we talk?"

"Yeah, I think that would be a good idea." Maggie dropped her purse onto her desk. "Brian told me what happened last night with you two." Her friend hardly needed to state the obvious. Concern poured from her friend's eyes.

She dropped into a chair as relief washed over her. It was going to be okay. Maggie would convince Brian not to take the job.

"The assignment is for only a year." Maggie took her hand. "He could Skype you every day and you'd have the kids and me to keep you company."

"I know." Tears pricked the back of her eyes, knowing she had friends she could count on. If only loneliness was her greatest concern. Being on her own didn't even rank in the top ten of her worries. "Brian being in harm's way terrifies me."

"Danger goes with the territory. It's simply a calculated risk that goes with the job."

Riley shook her head. "I don't see how you can be so calm. He could die."

"That's true, but that's not going to change anything." Maggie's words took on an imploring tone. "Right now, what he needs is for you to be strong. He needs to know you'll be waiting for him when he gets back. Don't underestimate what that means to us when we're out there on a mission."

More than anything in the world, Riley wished she were strong enough for him, that she could smile bravely and say all the right words. She clenched the chair's armrests, wishing she could suck back the fear churning inside her. Problem was she'd been there and done that, playing the role of supportive spouse. Because of that she knew she couldn't go that route again. Just revisiting the constant worry in her imagination was enough to send her into a full-blown panic attack.

She pegged Maggie with a look she hoped conveyed her feelings better than her feeble words. "I love your brother, but I can't put myself through that again." Guilt tore at her soul, but it was the truth.

Maggie snatched her hands from Riley's grasp. "I

can't believe you'd be so self-centered." Anger turned her face scarlet. "This isn't about you. This is about you sucking it up and being there for someone who needs you."

Even as Riley searched for an explanation, memories of Jake's death ran on an endless loop. The appearance of Jake's supervisor at her door, viewing her husband's bloody body, it was all there as fresh as it was three years ago. "Not self-centeredness, self-preservation."

"You really surprise me. I thought you were better than that."

Riley jerked her chin upward as if she'd been slapped. She'd been a fool to think these people were her friends. Despite Maggie's assurance that she'd be there for Riley, these were Brian's people, not hers. "I'm sorry to disappoint you." She stood. There was nothing left to say. The lines were drawn, and once again she stood on the outside looking in. As old wounds reopened, her coping mechanism for the pain roared to life.

If I work through the night, I can get my things packed and be on the road out of town by tomorrow morning. Her feet kept moving past her cubicle, leading her towards Grant's office. "I need a minute of your time."

He looked up from the computer. "What's up?"

Riley tamped down on her emotions, pushing aside Maggie's rejection. She'd have plenty of time to give them full rein later. She forced her thoughts on what she needed to say to her boss. "I'm turning in my notice, effective immediately."

He pushed back from his desk. "I told you if

Heather made you an offer to please give me the opportunity to give you a better one."

"She didn't. I just can't stay."

Grant came around to the front of his desk. "What did my meathead friend do?"

"Nothing." There was no way she could endure having another person turn on her. "It's just time for me to move on."

He crossed his arms. "I'm not buying that for a minute. I saw the way you two were yesterday." His gaze locked on to hers. "I also saw the look on your face when Brainstorm made his announcement. Not one of his smartest moves. But you know he'll be as careful as he can, don't you?"

"Yeah." Promises he didn't have the power to keep despite his intentions. "And Maggie assured me it was part of life in the military."

He let out a breath. "I'm sure she did." Then he reached for his phone. "Before you go running off, let me do something for you."

She looked at him through tear clouded eyes. "You don't owe me anything."

"The hell I don't. You matter here, even if not everyone can see that now." His gaze shot to the door behind her.

"You've been good to me. Better than I expected considering." After Maggie's reaction, she expected to be run out of Magnolia Springs on a rail.

"Are you kidding me? I'd be afraid to sleep tonight if Abby knew I hadn't done everything humanly possible for you." He stared down at her, his blue eyes radiating warmth she desperately needed. "Let me give Heather a call and let her know you're going to be making contact with her."

As much as she wanted to run, she didn't have that luxury. "Thank you." At least she didn't have to worry about finding another job.

"No problem." He punched in the number. "Besides, I don't want you getting too far away. I have a feeling things are going to work out for you and my meathead friend."

She shook her head. "I wish I had your optimism."

Chapter Seventeen

Riley turned down the administrative wing at Mountain View Resort, hoping she wouldn't have to double back or duck into a restroom. This wasn't her first attempt to make the short commute between the suite where she now resided and her new office. She'd already been sick twice that morning. Neither was this the only morning nausea had been her alarm clock. Hopefully, the ginger ale and soda crackers she'd grabbed from the kitchen would help settle her stomach. Riley had just tucked the packet of crackers into her desk drawer when Heather Davis popped her head in the door.

"You feeling better today?"

"Much." The lie pricked her conscience as a surge of gratitude flooded her already overloaded emotions. She lucked out that the woman still needed her after she'd turned down the offer several times. "Must have been something I ate." She tried not to think about food at all. She had too much on her plate to be sick, too much in fact to do anything but attend to the dozens of tasks she needed to complete. *Thank Goodness.*

As for lying to her new boss, the reason for her ailment wasn't something Heather needed to worry about. Grief wasn't contagious. When she'd lost Jake, her body had responded similarly with a heavy feeling in her chest and muscle aches. Although then, she hadn't been sick to her stomach or had an aversion to eating anything that wasn't clear liquids and dry crackers.

Trying to divert her thoughts from Brian, she powered up her computer. "I've filled all the openings for the spa and I've scheduled interviews for the golf and tennis pro positions for Monday."

The job proved more than an entry level position. She oversaw Mountain View's amenities, hired workers, and supervised staff, enough work to keep her busy at least eighty hours out of the week. Not that Brian was ever far from her thoughts. His face played on an endless loop in the back of her mind. But at lease she didn't have to face Maggie's censorious stare every day.

"Awesome." Heather stepped inside the room. "Come next spring, this place is going to finally be on the map. You've been a tremendous help, practically a miracle worker."

"Hardly." The woman proved an easy person to work for. "It's just a matter of diving in. Besides, I like keeping busy." Even as she said the words, her chest tightened. She drew in a deep breath. Hopefully, well before next spring she'd be past the grief. Despite attempting to protect her heart from loss, part of her died when she'd walked away from Brian.

"But I don't want to run you off. We've got time to get all this done."

Under different circumstances Riley might have allowed herself to consider the woman a friend. Not after the experience she'd had with Maggie. Riley would never mistake an easy-going management style for friendship. This was a professional arrangement amenable to them both. Heather got what she needed, a competent employee, and Riley got free room and board. "I don't mind. It's not like I've got a family waiting at home for me." She glanced at the calendar on her desk. "Aren't you getting Grace today?" Part of Riley's duties also included acting as manager on duty the days Heather had her daughter.

She shook her head. "I forgot to tell you. I wanted to be here for the Latimer/ Hogan wedding tomorrow and since Grant and Abby will be attending as well, Aunt Katie's watching her." She patted Riley's arm. "Were you planning to attend?"

Since taking the job two weeks ago this wedding had loomed on the horizon. "No." The word jumped from her lips with more force than necessary. "I didn't know Lindsey that well." There was no way she was ready to face the people she'd grown to care about. "Besides, I've still got tons to do here."

Riley gripped the edge of her desk as a wave of nausea washed over her. Would Brian still go? Probably not since he hadn't been too keen on attending in the first place. But she couldn't risk it. Seeing him would shatter her. She took a few steadying breaths. Most days she was barely keeping her head above water, and not because of the amount of work her new job required. While walking away from Brian had been one of the hardest things she'd ever done, it was the right thing for both of them. But God, she missed him.

"You should go."

Riley shrugged. "That's okay. If you don't need me, I'd like to take the day off." Rest was the last thing she wanted, though after two non-stop weeks her body was screaming for rest.

Heather cocked her head, studying her more than she was comfortable with. "I think Maggie and Brian will be there."

The woman's statement had her wondering what Grant had told his ex. Not much by the way she accepted Riley's faked nonchalance. "I'd rather spend a quiet day reading."

"Suit yourself," She rose from her seat. "But I'm sure everyone would love to see you."

Riley sincerely doubted that was the case.

****

Brian stared at the jumble of odds and ends he kept in his top dresser drawer trying to remember what he was supposed to be doing. One look at the box containing Riley's engagement ring and his brain went offline.

Maggie leaned against the door frame. "You know no one would fault you if you stayed home."

After a couple weeks training in Tucson, he was home for the weekend. From here on, the length of time he'd be away would get longer until come January he'd be in country full time. This was the last opportunity to his family and friends for a while.

"I'm going. It's not like I've got anything better to do." He pushed aside the ring box in favor of the tie he been searching for.

If he was smart, he would be kicking back with a cold beer instead of tying a noose around his neck. Then again, no one had ever accused him of being a smart man, despite his moniker. With the chance he could see Riley, Mountain View called to him. Not that he held any hope of changing her mind. Quitting her job and leaving town sent a clear message. But as she had from the first time he laid eyes on her, he was drawn to Riley with a need that bordered on desperation.

"Boy, you're a glutton for punishment. The kids and I will be waiting in the family room."

He thought back to his youth, to the times his old man pounded the crap out of him. Back then he hadn't known when to give up either. No matter how bad the beatings he'd kept coming after his old man until the General was too tired to pound him anymore.

He couldn't leave for South America without one last glimpse, maybe even get a chance to say goodbye. How was he going to pull that off? Brian normally didn't leave the house without a plan. It was one of the things that made him good at his job. If you were going to move thousands of troops and tons of equipment, a guy needed to think ahead.

Brian didn't have a clue what he was doing as he palmed the ring box. Clearly, a ring wasn't going to change the fact he was about to head into a dangerous situation in South America. Or make Riley willing to accept the burden that went along with being the one left behind.

Maybe he should just forget about going. So many things could happen to turn his good intentions into a cluster fuck. He started to call out to Maggie but something stopped him. The last time he'd just winged it was the day after his first workout with Riley, when he'd been convinced things would never work out between them. While he'd been right about that much, he didn't regret showing up at her house. Or, what happened afterward. Listening to his gut, Brian slipped the ring in his pocket.

An hour later, Brian followed Maggie and the kids into the ballroom where the ceremony was taking place. From the moment they'd driven onto the property, he started scanning for Riley. Instead, Grant caught his attention. The guy cocked an eyebrow before stalking over.

"I'm on my best behavior." He'd already heard from his buddy how much he'd messed up in the way he'd handled his announcement.

"You are going to try to talk to her, aren't you?"

"No, he's not." Maggie elbowed her business partner. "She made her position perfectly clear. He's better off without her."

Maggie's treatment of Riley was a source of continued animosity between his sister and him. While he appreciated her sense of loyalty, she hadn't earned the wrath of Mad Dog Magdalena. "I'm over my friends and family interfering in my life. I can fuck things up all by myself thank you." With that he walked up the aisle, taking a seat as the wedding music began.

The next several minutes were about as close to torture as you could get without whipping out the bamboo skewers. Between cotton-candy bunting, syrupy wedding songs, and the deeply sincere vows the couple exchanged, Brian was in danger of slipping into a diabetic coma. As he watched the newlyweds walk arm in arm up the aisle, an old army adage came to mind. *If the army had wanted its soldiers to have wives, it would have issued them.*

Brian thought to the job ahead of him. There'd be weeks when he was in the field where he wouldn't be reachable. Maybe Riley was right. Putting her in a situation like that wasn't fair. Not that it would be a problem now. Maggie and the kids would be fine on their own. And so would he eventually.

Wading hip deep into the situation in South America might push the longing for Riley to manageable levels. He bet once he really got in the thick of things, she'd only cross his mind every half hour instead of the constant loop of her beautiful face that played in the background.

But for now, he was willing to suffer the pain he'd feel, so he could say a proper goodbye. After the ceremony, Brian milled about the ballroom pretending to mingle. While he shook hands and made small talk, he searched for a glimpse of dark hair. Leaving his sister and friend behind, he was about to slip out one of the ballrooms side doors when he felt a hand on his arm.

"I haven't seen you in a coon's age." A cousin on his mother's side gave him a hug.

****

The quiet knock on her door pulled Riley's attention from her book. As she crossed the suite for the door, her feet sank into the plush taupe-colored carpet. Her digs at Mountain View were comfortable and met her simple needs, but she missed the bare floors and sunny walls of her house back in Magnolia Springs.

"Sorry to bother you." It was Ana, a middle-age Latina who filled the position of Heather's administrative assistant. "Ms. Davis said she needs you in her office. It seems the groom has a special request."

So much for hiding out. "It's no problem. Give me a couple minutes."

After putting on the light green blouse and navy-blue skirt that made up the senior staff's uniform, she slipped through the corridors, hoping not to run into anyone she knew. She met Heather in the hall outside her office. "I hate doing this to you after I promised you a day off."

Riley waved away the apology. "What's going on?"

"The groom saw your car in the employee parking lot and would like to take some of the wedding photos with it." She sounded hopeful as she continued. "At first I said no, but now I'm wondering if you'd mind."

Riley smiled, remembering Lindsey saying how much her fiancé loved old cars. "Tell Travis, I'd be glad for him to take Gloria's picture. I'll go right now and drop her top."

After pulling the convertible around to the front of the hotel, she was free to return to her suite. As several hundred guests milled about in front of the ballroom, the chances of her running into someone she knew grew by the minute. Instead of heading to her first-floor rooms, she walked to the employees' entrance to the ball room. There was no guarantee Brian would attend the wedding of his buddy's daughter, but deep in her heart she hoped if he had come, she might catch a glimpse of him.

Riley peeked through the glass embedded in the swinging door, quickly locking on his head of dark blond hair. Greedy for the sight of him, what she'd intended to be a quick look turned into an all-encompassing stare.

He stood stiff and erect with those around him, ever the soldier even out of uniform. This comforted her. Perhaps if he was as vigilant with his safety as he was his military bearing, he'd be okay during his time in South America.

Quickly, she pushed that notion aside. Nothing guaranteed his safety short of him staying here on American soil. That firm truth was why the two of them were separated by the door she now used as a shield.

Finally, several of the guests parted and she was able to get a better glimpse of him.

At the sight of his full mouth and chiseled jaw her resolve weakened, especially when he bent to whisper something in Matt's ear that made him laugh. She still loved him, probably always would. She wanted nothing more in the world than to beg his forgiveness.

She pushed against the door, stepping into the ballroom. She'd worked up enough courage to say hello. Then perhaps if that went well, she'd ask to meet for coffee.

A lovely woman, mid-forties with nice curves and pretty hair, sidetracked Riley's plans when she sidled up to Brian with comfort born of familiarity. He smiled, then twined one arm around the woman's waist before pressing his lips to her cheek.

The kiss felt like a blow. She drew in a breath against the pain of knowing she'd meant so little that she could be replaced so soon. It shouldn't have surprised her. She'd been a part of his life for such a short time and he had every right to be with whomever he wanted. Especially if he could find someone who met his needs the way she hadn't been able to.

As if he'd sensed her gaze, Brian turned, jerking his head in her direction. His eyes widened as their gazes connected. Turning on one heel, she fled the room, racing down the corridor and brushing tears from her eyes.

"Riley, stop."

If she'd had any kind of backbone, she'd have let him catch up with her. At the moment, she was in full survival mode and needed to be away from this damnable place more than she needed her next breath. Acting solely on instinct, she doubled back to the front entrance where she'd parked Gloria. Before she could plan a destination, she was out of the parking lot.

****

Brian ran after Riley, rushing down one corridor after another until he lost her. Again. The knowledge he'd let her slip through his grasp cut as freshly as it had when she'd disappeared from his life two weeks before. He stopped with his hand on the door of the ballroom, mostly to delay the moment when he'd have to explain why he'd taken off.

Then distant sirens caught his attention. When a fire truck joined the shriller cry of a police cruiser, he figured some unfortunate soul had been broadsided at the intersection half a mile away. The yocals needed to get their act together and put up better signage. This wasn't the country anymore where everyone knew the roads. When the sound of an ambulance joined the noise, Brian's senses kicked into overdrive. Something bad had happened, and it called to him when he should have walked in the opposite direction. In seconds he was inside his truck and barreling down the resort's drive.

What he found at the intersection turned his blood to shards of ice. He forced the truck to the side of the road, kicking up gravel and narrowly missing the guardrail. Why should he care about safety? The worst had already happened. Riley's car lay in a crumpled heap at the bottom of a pile of medal and glass. He raced forward, her name a roar escaping his mouth.

Two First Responders blocked his trajectory. "Hold up, buddy. They're trying to work over there."

"Is anyone hurt?"

"Yeah, one pretty bad." The officer grabbed Brian's shoulders when he tried to sidestep the guy. "Which is why you need to stay out of their way."

Brian pointed to Riley's convertible. "I know the driver. Is she the one who's hurt?"

The cop looked over his shoulder at the tangled cars. Then he shot Brian a look that screamed, *what do you think?* The red convertible was wrapped around the grille of a SUV, broken nearly in half by the oversized monster. The only saving grace to the situation was impact had been on the passenger side.

Brian's relief was short-lived as the paramedics wheeled a stretcher towards the wreckage. He pushed against the cop, needing to see how badly she was hurt.

"That's close enough."

Brian tamped down on the urge to take his frustrations out of the guy who had him by the shoulders. The paramedics eased her from the car, a neck brace already in place. They strapped her to a backboard. Blood covered her face and arms. Impotent raged filled him as they loaded her in the waiting ambulance. "Where are you taking her?"

"Are you a relative?"

"She doesn't have any family." The truth tore at him. Through no fault of hers, she was alone.

The cop hesitated, seeming to struggle whether to give Brian the information. "Magnolia Springs Regional is the closest trauma center."

Chapter Eighteen

Please let her be okay.

It had been so many years since Brian prayed, he wasn't sure God had any interest in listening. He wasn't going to risk leaving anything to chance. Living in a world where Riley didn't exist was untenable. If he needed to light a church-full of candles, offer a burnt sacrifice, or make a truckload of promises he'd do it. Whatever it took.

Don't let it end like this.

Riley deserved a long, happy life and to die at a hundred-ten, surrounded by family and friends. Not alone and way too soon.

Back at the accident scene, fear like he'd never known before set up shop in his gut and hours later the fight or flight urges still lingered. With nothing to fight and nowhere to run, his emotions were a powder keg.

"Can I get you some coffee or something to eat?" Maggie asked.

Brian lifted his head from his palms. "I'm good." He scanned the hospital waiting room. Besides his sister, Grant, Abby, and about half the Mountain View staff was camped out with him.

Maggie gripped his shoulder. "Why don't you go home for a while? You've been here all night."

Riley had been in surgery for hours. It didn't matter how long he had to wait, he wasn't going anywhere until he'd knew she was okay. After that, he'd leave her in peace. Lord knew he'd caused her enough grief already. "I. Am. Not. Leaving. Her." His roar caught everyone's attention.

Maggie flinched, giving him another reason for self-loathing. Riley's accident rested solidly on his shoulders. If he had stayed at home, she wouldn't have gotten in her car and fled.

"Sorry. I'm crawling the walls here." He stared at the double doors leading to the nurses' station and patient rooms, willing them to open. "What's taking so long?" Long was not good. Long surgeries equaled bad outcomes. Life altering outcomes.

Maggie patted his shoulder again, doing her best to keep him calm. "The nurse said they'd send someone out as soon as they had something to share."

Brian nodded, thinking back to the accident that cost him his legs. And the lives of two of his best men. Had Maggie been this calm waiting to hear his fate? Or had she needed the shoulder of her business partner, Grant? How had they stood the uncertainty of not knowing if he'd survived the explosion?

Prior to his accident, Brian had never thought about his mortality or been overly concerned with safety, and practically everyone he knew did something dangerous. Even Maggie flew cargo planes at night and over long distances. While he cared about the people in his life, he'd never especially worried about them getting hurt. Nothing like falling in love to give a guy a different perspective.

The double doors finally opened after what seemed an eternity, sending everyone in the room to their feet. Brian reached the woman clad in faded pink scrubs first. "Can you give us an update on Riley Logan?"

He didn't realize he'd latched onto the nurse until she looked down where he had a grip on her wrist. He forced his palm open.

The woman folded her arms across her chest. "Are you her next of kin?"

"We're her friends." Grant spread on the charm. *Thank fuck,* since it seemed Brian was intent on pissing people off. "We'd appreciate anything you can tell us about her condition." Grant used that persuasive tone of his that got folks to do whatever he wanted.

"I'll see what I can do. But for now, we have to wait until she's conscious and can give her consent to talk to you." The woman left them, walking away at a brisk clip.

Then miracle of miracles, the blessed angel of mercy was back within minutes. "I can't tell you any specifics about your friend, but I can say Dr. Patel is monitoring her patient in recovery."

"Thank you." He wanted to hug the nurse for her efforts. "Would you ask the doctor to come talk to us when she gets a chance? I think her family should be here in the next little while." Brian added a smile to his request as his mind raced with ideas. Knowing Riley was stable had taken the edge off his fears, but he wasn't ready to leave by any stretch of the imagination.

Brian eyed the keypad, watching as the nurse punched in the code to gain access to the patient area. He wasn't going to let something as trivial as HIPPA laws keep him from Riley.

Grant came to stand next to him. "That will only get you thrown out," he said just loud enough for Brian to hear.

"I know." He moved his suit jacket he'd shed hours ago and slumped into the hard-plastic chair. Waking up after his accident and seeing Maggie had meant the world to him. He'd be damned if Riley was going to wake up alone, even if he had to get sneaky to make that happen. Or creative, he thought as he felt the ring box in his jacket pocket.

When a petite lady dressed a long white coat came into view he was ready. "Dr. Patel, I'm hoping you have some good news for us." Brian imitated his best friend, gently shaking the doctor's hand and smiling like a fool.

"Are you family?"

"I'm her fiancé." He dared the peanut gallery behind him to say otherwise.

His gaze was met by several pairs of wide eyes, but thankfully they all kept their pie holes shut. "I have her ring here." Brian held up his hand, showing the solitaire he'd pushed down on his pinky finger.

Dr. Patel moved to the corner of the waiting room and spoke in a low voice. "Your fiancée is a lucky woman. Things could have been much worse. I did have to remove her spleen to control the bleeding, but I expect her to make a full recovery."

Brian let out a breath, his energy leaving him along with the spent air. "Thank God. When can I see her?"

"They're moving her to a room. You can go as soon as they have her settled."

He pumped the air in triumph. "She's going to be okay. I'll let you know when she wakes up."

The nurses were exiting the room as he arrived. He'd prepared himself for the likelihood she'd be bandaged and that there'd be an IV, a heart monitor, and maybe even a respirator. Considering he'd seen far worse back in the hospital in Germany, his legs shouldn't have suddenly lost the ability to hold him upright.

Nothing he'd ever experienced prepared him for the sight of her slender body barely lifting the sheet covering her. Besides the large bandage on her forehead, she'd also lost all the color that made her seem vibrant, healthy.

Brian did something he hadn't since he was a kid, he cried. He buried his face in his hands and lost it. Relief flooded him, followed quickly by the desire to never experience that level of fear again. Now he knew what Riley had talked about. Having faced the possibility of a world without her in it, he couldn't imagine living through that fear again.

Nor could he envision living without her. Drawing in a breath, he got his shit together. He crossed the room, pulling a chair to her bedside. Brian tugged the ring from his finger and stretching across Riley's sleeping body, he slipped the diamond on her hand.

Brian brushed his thumb over her knuckles. *Damn, that ring looked right on her hand.* Hopefully, when Riley woke, she'd think the same thing. All kinds of happily ever after plans poured through his mind. Screw the Mobletech job. He'd dig ditches or work at a fast-food joint if that was what it took to build a secure future for her. If someone told him six months ago he'd be considering marriage, he'd have said they'd been smoking dope on the back forty. But there he was, making plans that included him doing whatever it took to keep that ring on Riley's finger.

Now that he'd laid eyes on her and seen his worst

fears weren't realized, the hours keeping vigil caught up to him. After pulling up a chair, Brian rested his head against the hospital bed and let sleep overtake him. Sometime later, he awoke when her hand stroked against his head. Having been deprived of her touch, he reveled in the soothing sensation.

"How you feeling?" He searched her face for signs of pain.

"Too early…to tell."

"Do you need anything?"

She shook her head and then drifted off again.

He watched over her as she rested, taking in every bruise and cut on her beautiful face. She woke several times over the next few hours, but mostly she slept. When the nurses came in to check her vitals, they assured him it was normal for patients to sleep a good bit after surgery.

Towards the twelve hour mark her eyes opened and stayed that way for more than a few moments. Her brow furrowed.

"Are you in pain?

Her gaze shifted to the assortment of medical equipment around her. "How bad am I?"

If anyone asked him, a hangnail was too much for her to endure.

Especially as the accident was his fault. If only he'd stayed at home, not returned for the second workout session with her, or any of the other decisions he'd made in the last few months. But he had, and now it was his duty to see she never knew another moment of distress.

As his gaze worked over her myriad of tiny cuts and bruises, the need to make her world right twisted his gut and cut off his words. Brian had to clear his throat before he could speak. "I've seen worse."

Her wounds would heal soon enough, as hopefully would the worries that kept them apart. Back in the waiting room while he'd been making bargains with the Almighty, he'd promised that if she was okay he'd walk away from her. Now leaving wasn't an option. At this point he'd be willing to give up anything to get her back.

She offered him a weak smile.

Brian grasped her hand, bringing it to his lips. "You scared the shit out of me. Don't ever do that again." The irony of his words wasn't lost on him now that he stood in Riley's shoes.

She licked her lips then hoarsely whispered. "Okay."

Eager for something concrete he could do to ease her pain, he went into the bathroom to wet a washcloth. As he brought the cloth to her dry lips, she clasped his hand and in doing so caused her ring to catch the light. Her gaze latched on to her hand.

"I told the doctor I was your fiancé. I couldn't risk them not letting me in to see you. It was presumptuous of me to put it on your finger. But…"

She opened her mouth.

"Don't try to talk. Just listen."

Her nod elicited a grimace.

Brian cocked his hip against the bed, needing to get closer. "Riley, I love you so much," he said, wishing he'd worked out ahead a time what he'd say. "For someone who's faced danger all his life, I find I can face anything but the loss of you."

Their eyes met for a moment before she looked

away. *God, he was making a mess of this.* "What if I didn't take the job in South America, would you give me a second chance?"

Several seconds past with only the sound of his heart pounding to fill the silence. A tear trickled down her cheek. "I can't." She clenched her eyes. "I can't ask you to do that."

"Yes, you can, and I'd gladly do it for you."

She met and held his gaze. "I know, but that isn't what you need. If you walk away from this job, you're always going to wonder what might have been. Tears pooled in her beautiful violet eyes, darkening them to a deep purple. "In the long run, you'd come to resent me as well." With great effort, she tugged the ring from her finger, holding it out to him with a hand that shook. "Let's admit to ourselves, that we aren't right for each other."

Brian couldn't bring himself to take the ring. He couldn't when every cell in his body disagreed with her. Riley Logan was the best goddamned thing to ever happen to him.

Clearly, the reverse wasn't true. Even as they were once again at this impasse, he was making life more difficult for her. He could no more bring anxiety and hardship to her life than he could hurt Matt and Lexi or be disloyal to his country. It was time to let her go. God, even the thought killed him.

At least his prayers had been answered. She was alive and in no time she'd thrive in the life she was building for herself. He stood. "All right then."

When he reached the door, he turned back for one last look. "Take care."

****

With those two words he was gone. The snick of the door as it closed sounded like a tomb closing.

You too.

Although she doubted he would. He was wide open and reckless and thought little of his personal safety. She'd done the right thing for herself. And for him. He deserved someone stronger, someone who could wait without conjuring up a worst-case scenario. She wasn't that person.

With Brian gone, she let the steady stream of tears loose until sobs racked her body. Her emotional wounds bled into her physical ones, the two joining until they became a force she could no longer fight. She curled in a ball, letting the pain take over. Her brain screamed for relief after a few minutes, but she beat back the urge to grab the plunger to the pain pump someone placed within reach. Instead, she pushed the thing off the edge of the bed. She didn't deserve an escape from pain considering the injuries she inflicted on the man she loved.

Minutes later at the sound of the door opening, Riley swallowed her sobs. She turned to face the doctor she vaguely remembered from the Recovery Room. "My word." The woman rushed to her bedside and placed the plunger in Riley's hand. "You're going to heal faster if you're not in so much pain, and I'd like you to be comfortable while we talk."

She relented, pressing the button which shot a dose of medicine into the IV line. After a few moments, the doctor patted her on the leg. "That won't take but a minute to kick in." Then she flipped open the chart she carried under her arm. "I have a couple developments I didn't discuss with you back in Recovery. You might want your fiancé to hear them as well. Would you like me to ask him to come back in?"

The doctor's ominous words helped Riley beat back the drowsiness warming her muscles and fogging her brain. So did the reminder of Brian's fib. "He's not…" Unable to finish the sentence or look into the kind eyes of her doctor, she clenched her eyes. "No, he's gone."

"Okay then." Dr. Patel smiled. "I've got good news and better news. Which do you want first?"

At the moment she would have settled for news that didn't suck. "Either one."

"As I told you in Recovery, I took out your spleen. There's been no sign of infection, and you'll be sore for a few days, but there's no reason you can't be back on your feet in a couple weeks."

"That's good." She could go back to work soon.

The doctor continued her cheery news, despite Riley's lackluster response. "The better news is no harm was done to the fetus in the accident. You're early enough in the pregnancy, so your baby was protected inside your body."

****

Riley's head pounded as that golden word "baby" echoed in her mind. She'd wanted the chance to be a mom since she was a kid herself. The cruel mistake added to her pain. "I think you need to check the name on that chart. I can't get pregnant." How much more would she have to endure before her heart broke or her mind snapped?

"I did and you are." The doctor sat on the edge of the bed. "I take it you didn't know."

Shaking her head was all she could manage. She

clung to the first glimmer of hope she'd had in weeks. If she couldn't have Brian at least she could have a part of him. "Please tell me you're sure of this."

"We could do an ultrasound, if you like."

"Please." She wouldn't let herself hope as she waited for the staff to wheel in the machine. Just kept telling herself it was a medical mix-up. Someone in the lab must have switched the pregnancy tests. All through the prep she reminded herself of the months of fertility treatments and the disappointments she and Jake had faced. As the technician fired up the monitor, Riley turned her face away. With her eyes screwed down tight, she waited for the technician to confirm what she already knew.

The young woman scooted the probe over her belly. "There's the little peanut."

Her heart skipped. "Is it okay?" she asked, unable to get her head around the fact there was a baby growing inside her much less fathom that she'd soon have a son or daughter.

The technician moved the probe around some more. "Why don't you see for yourself?"

Riley's eyes latched onto the thumb-sized human before tears clouded her view. "I just can't believe it." Both the miracle growing in secret and that her little one would reveal itself on the day she most needed something precious to cling to. "I've wanted this for so long."

"I'm very happy for you." She cleaned the gel off her stomach. "Rest well and don't hesitate to ring the nurses' call button if you need anything."

"I will." Although short of an easy way of breaking the news to Brian, she couldn't think of anything else she could need.

As she worked through the words she'd say to him, she clung to the sonogram picture the technician left. After a nap, she'd call. Then as soon as she was released from the hospital she'd make the trip down to Magnolia Springs. The least he deserved was a face to face meeting when she broke the news. But that would have to keep for a few hours. Riley drifted off to sleep, hoping he'd want to be part of her baby's life.

Her first instinct when she opened her eyes was to reach for the sonogram picture. Having done the same each time she woke during the night, the sight of her little peanut still brought happy tears to her eyes.

"Right." She geared up for the tasks ahead. During her second day in the hospital she'd been able to sit up in the bed and keep down a few ice chips. Though she wanted a shower desperately, she had to accomplish her milestones one at a time. Those were the easy tasks. She also had to place that call to Brian. Eyeing the darkened window in her tiny hospital room, she figured that conversation should wait till the sun came up. The door opened seconds after she pressed the call button. "That was quick. I was wondering when…"

As she sat up in bed, her world once again tipped on its ear. Brian eased inside her room as if he expected her to still be asleep. "Should you be doing that?"

Her breath caught. Still dressed in the suit he'd worn to the wedding and with a deep shadow covering his jaw and underneath his eyes, it was plain he hadn't left the hospital. Equally evident by the pounding in her chest was the hold he had on her. She had to grip the bed rails to keep from holding her arms out to him. "What are you doing here?"

"I got as far as the end of the hall and my feet wouldn't go any further."

Her mind played over all the times she thought she'd run far enough to escape her feelings for him, or ruined things by saying something stupid. Every time he came back. He'd never once abandoned her. Fresh tears burned at the back of her eyes.

He let out a breath. "I only wanted to look in on you."

When he turned to go, she summoned her courage for the conversation ahead. "Stay. Just for a minute."

The corner of his mouth turned up. "Anything you need, sunshine." He crossed the room but stopped short of her reach.

As always, that seed of fear crept into her thoughts, cautioning her that he might not welcome the news. For once she was able to ignore what might happen. Brian deserved to know she was having his baby.

Squeezing her eyes closed, she prayed for the right words. Nothing seemed adequate to express the hopes she had that he'd want to play even a small role in their baby's life.

When she couldn't find her voice, he asked, "Is something the matter? Are you hurting? I could get the nurse."

She drew comfort in the nearly frantic way he hurried to ease her. Surely if he cared enough to see to her comfort after all the pain she'd caused him, he'd have room in his heart for an innocent baby. "I'm fine. Really fine." She stilled his hand when he reached for the call button. "I got some good news. At least it's good for me, and I hope you'll think it's good as well." She met his gaze. "Listen, this doesn't have to change anything unless you want it to. I mean I can totally handle things if you don't want to be a part."

He stroked her cheek. "Riley, baby, you're not making much sense." Worry lines creased the corners of his eyes. "Be a part of what?"

She swallowed hard, and then uttered the words she never thought she'd get to say. "I'm pregnant."

Brian blinked several times. Then swallowed. And again, his Adam's apple working overtime. "You're…"

"I didn't think I could." She squeezed his hand. "Please don't be angry. I honestly thought I couldn't get pregnant. Jake and I tried for years." Her voice climbed an octave with each sentence.

"Shhh." He stroked her hair like she was a skittish animal.

She didn't hold out hope that he'd still want her, didn't misinterpret his gentle caresses. She'd hurt him too many times. "I know this is a shock."

His lips formed the sweetest smile she'd ever seen, and the kiss he placed on the back of her hand soothed her in a way she had no right to expect. "Yes, it is a shock but a good one. The second-best thing you could ever tell me." Brian cupped her chin. "The first would be that you still wanted me."

She did. With every breath. Her soul, her body, with every part of her, she wanted him. "I never stopped." Her past was such a dark place. A place she was tired of living in. She wanted to move forward. Forward to a life filled with love and joy. She could see what she wanted, almost reach out and grab it. All that stood between her and that goal was the fear she'd let rule her life.

"But… But nothing." Her heart pounded. "Kiss

me." She tilted her head, offering her mouth.

His lips sealed over hers. Urgency laced each stroke until they were both panting when he broke the kiss to say, "I mean it, Riley. I'll call Colonel Weston this second if that's what it takes. There's nothing I won't give up for you." His hand brushed lightly across her stomach. "For our child. The only thing I would ever regret was letting you go."

In that moment she first began to believe. Not only he'd return home safely, but that she was strong enough to wait while he did something important. "With growing this little one to keep me busy and knowing you'd move heaven and earth to come back to us, I think I might be brave enough to let you go."

Brian shook his head. "I won't ask you to do that."

No, but it was something she could offer. Riley buried her face in the curve of his neck, absorbing his strength as his arms fenced her. After a moment she looked up at him. "Not that I'm anxious to get rid of you but I think this might be something we both need." Then she drew in a breath, knowing she was right. "It might actually put both our pasts to rest."

****

Brian's mind swam as things took an unexpected one-eighty. "Let me get this straight. You want me to take this job even though there's a chance I could get hurt again."

She nodded, her expression softening as she spoke. "I get it now. You and I both need to know we're stronger than the blows fate dealt us. Coming out the other side of this job will prove that."

"Good God, woman. You are…" Words failed him. "You constantly amaze me." He brought his mouth to hers. As did the depth of her strength.

She gripped his nape while offering him feather-light kisses. "A year is such a short period when you consider how many we have ahead of us." Then she looked up at him from her dark lashes. "Years in which I fully intend on giving you all the love, joy, and smart-ass comebacks you richly deserve." Her face lit in the first genuine smile he'd seen in weeks.

He'd take it, by God, every one of her snarky comebacks. Riley deserved some things from him in return. His gaze landed on the ring still lying where he'd left it the day before. Reaching for it, he sent up a prayer for the right words. "You've already made me the happiest SOB on earth just by being alive. It would be my great honor if you would consent to be my wife." He waited, not daring to assume anything. Thankfully, she didn't leave him hanging for long.

"It's me who's honored." Tears shimmered in her eyes. "After what I put you through."

He put the ring on her finger. As the diamond slid in place, so did all the pieces of his life. Making him thankful for all he'd endured in the last eighteen months, since it brought him to this moment. And now that he was here, there wasn't anything he wouldn't do to return to this exact spot, wrapped up in his woman's love. "Just goes to show what a stubborn mule I am." After pressing a kiss to her fingers, he tilted her chin. "Whatever it takes, I'll get back to you and our child."

Riley squeezed her eyelids, causing tears to run down her face. "I'm going to cling to that every time I get scared for you."

Brian let out a breath. "Now we have that settled, you need to rest." He urged her to lie back on the bed.

While her color had improved since he saw her the day before, she still looked like a stiff wind would knock her over.

She pulled the covers up her shoulders as she closed her eyes. "I feel much better, actually. I was worried about telling you I was pregnant." She cracked an eyelid. "I didn't want you to think I'd lied or was manipulating you into staying."

The thought never crossed his mind. "You don't have a manipulative bone in your body," he assured her. He, however, wasn't above using her pregnancy to his advantage. He wanted to make her his in every way possible, as soon as possible. "You know if you want a big wedding, you're going to need to hurry with the planning." Not that he cared about the how and when. If he could get a justice of the peace, he'd marry Riley in the hospital's chapel. But maybe she wanted all the trimmings.

With her eyes closed, she shook her head. "I don't need that. I'm fine if we head to the courthouse the next time you're home on leave. It can even be just the two of us."

"I can make that happen." He hoped she wasn't saying that because she was unsure how his friends and family would react to their news. "Sleep for a bit and when you wake up we'll work out…"

The rest of his sentence was cut off when Maggie slipped through the door. "Oh, hi." Her gaze shot to his for a moment before settling on the bed where his and Riley's hands were joined. "I didn't know you'd be here."

Tension coiled up his spine. "Well, I am." His sister had many fine qualities, loyalty being one of them. The people in her life could count on her to have their backs no matter what. That tenacity also meant when people got on her shit list they stayed there. "I'm not going anywhere either." He loved Maggie. Nothing she did would change that, but he wasn't going to sit by and let her take a plug out of Riley.

Her chin jerked up as she crossed the room to stand at the foot of the bed. "That's fine. You both need to hear what I've got to say." She pulled her shoulders back. "I'm sorry for the pain I caused you both. I don't deserve it, but I hope with time you'll forgive me."

"Of course, I forgive you, Magpie." He opened his arms to her. Giving Riley's fingers a squeeze, he hoped she'd feel the same.

She proved him right as she reached for Maggie's hand. "There's nothing to forgive. I hurt your brother and you had a right to be mad."

Brian rolled his eyes. In seconds they were both doing that crying/laughing thing. He felt a little like tearing up himself. Considering where this nightmare started, he hardly knew what to do with all this happy, happy, happy. "So." The emotions were rubbing off on him. "There's more good news to go around."

"What?" Maggie thumbed away tears.

"I'm pregnant."

"She's pregnant."

Maggie's eyes widened as a smile split her face. "Really? I can't wait to tell Matt and Lexi. They'll be so pumped." She gripped his arm. "You're going to be the best dad in the whole world. I just know it."

Reality hit him with the force of a hammer.

I'm going to be some poor kid's old man.

Flashes of the past sent every nerve in his body

alight. The General had ruled rather than nurtured, punished mistakes rather than taught by example. Which left Brian with examples of what not to do.

Even as his head swam, determination steeled his spine. It didn't matter if he had to read every childrearing book ever written, he'd unlearn the parenting lessons he'd seen practiced by his own father. "I will. My kid deserves nothing less."

Maggie sat on the edge of the bed, taking Riley's free hand. "Will you come back to Davis Air Transport, please? The place hasn't been the same since you left."

God, there were so many details they had to work out, but one look at her let him know she'd been through enough for a while. "We'll figure that out in a couple days and let you know."

After hugging them both, she stood. "Good enough. I'll talk to you guys tomorrow."

Two minutes after Maggie left, Riley was out. He watched her sleep, counting her breaths and marveling at the changes this day had brought. Nurses came in to check her vitals and someone else brought in dinner. Eventually, the hours without sleep caught up to him and he laid his head against the bed. While he slept his brain created what he could only pray would one day come true. He was pushing a little dark-haired girl on a tire swing, and with every push she let out a giggle that still rang in his ears. More than the child's gender, the fact he was doing something that brought joy to her life was what had Brian waking with an ease he hadn't experienced in a long time.

Rubbing the sleep from his eyes he found Riley watching him. "Do you know the sex of the baby?"

"I think it's too early."

A germ of an idea took root, one he hoped she would go along with. If his dream turned out to be a prediction, his idea would bring them full circle.

"I know that look." The corner of her mouth crooked up. "What are you planning?"

"If it's a girl, I want us to name her Gloria."

Riley's eyebrows shot to her hairline, making him think he wasn't going to get his wish. "You want to name our daughter after a car?"

"Why not? She's what brought us together and I can't think of a better way to honor her efforts."

"Gloria it is, then."

They reached for each other, their arms twining together to form a bond nothing—not time, distance, nor even death-could separate. Sheltered between their bodies rested not only their unborn child, but their indestructible love.

A word about the author…

Melissa Klein writes southern fiction about everyday heroes fighting extraordinary battles. Whether facing the demands of caring for a child with special needs or the struggles of a soldier returning home, her characters take on the challenges life throws at them with perseverance, courage, and humor. Her favorite work-avoidance devices are gardening, pottery, reading, and playing with her grandsons.

While she won Georgia Romance Writers Unpublished Maggie award and Rose City Romance Writers Golden Rose award, she still hopes to win the lottery. If she does, she'll buy a huge farm in north Georgia and convince her children to live next door. Until that time, she lives in Atlanta with her husband and cat.

You can visit Melissa's website at www.melissakleinromance.com.

Thank you for purchasing
this publication of The Wild Rose Press, Inc.

For questions or more information
contact us at
info@thewildrosepress.com.

The Wild Rose Press, Inc.
www.thewildrosepress.com